Nothing Like You

Nothing Like You

Lauren Strasnick

Simon Pulse
New York London Toronto Sydney

SIMON PULSE
An imprint of Simon & Schuster Children's Publishing Division
1230 Avenue of the Americas, New York, NY 10020
First Simon Pulse hardcover edition October 2009
Copyright © 2009 by Lauren Strasnick
All rights reserved, including the right of reproduction in whole or in part in any form.
SIMON PULSE and colophon are registered trademarks of Simon & Schuster, Inc.
For information about special discounts for bulk purchases, please contact
Simon & Schuster Special Sales at 1-866-506-1949
or business@simonandschuster.com.
The Simon & Schuster Speakers Bureau can bring authors to your live event.
For more information or to book an event contact the Simon & Schuster Speakers
Bureau at 1-866-248-3049 or visit our website at www.simonspeakers.com.
Designed by Mike Rosamilia
The text of this book was set in Adobe Garamond.
Manufactured in the United States of America
2 4 6 8 10 9 7 5 3 1
Library of Congress Cataloging-in-Publication Data
Strasnick, Lauren.
Nothing like you / Lauren Strasnick. — 1st Simon Pulse hardcover ed.
p. cm.
Summary: Six months after her mother's death, seventeen-year-old Holly
finds some happiness in a secret affair with Paul, a boy she barely knows, but after
becoming friends with Paul's girlfriend, Saskia, Holly worries that her best friend,
Nils, or Saskia will learn the devastating truth.
ISBN 978-1-4169-8264-7
[1. Grief—Fiction. 2. Self-esteem—Fiction. 3. Sex—Fiction.
4. Friendship—Fiction. 5. High schools—Fiction. 6. Schools—Fiction.
7. Malibu (Calif.)—Fiction.] I. Title.
PZ7.S89787Not 2009
[Fic]—dc22
2008050092
ISBN 978-1-4169-8658-4 (eBook)

For Mameleh,
Mummy,
Caren,
Cookie,
Mom.
I miss you.

Nothing Like You

Chapter 1

We were parked at Point Dume, Paul and I, the two of us tangled together, half dressed, half not. Paul's car smelled like sea air and stale smoke, and from his rearview hung a yellow and pink plastic lanyard that swayed with the breeze drifting in through the open car window. I hung on to Paul, thinking, *I like your face, I love your hands, let's do this, let's do this, let's do this,* one arm locked around the back of his head, the other wedged between two scratched-up leather seat cushions, bracing myself against the pain while wondering, idly, if this feels any different when you love the person or when you do it lying down on a bed.

This was the same beach where I'd spent millions of mornings with my mother, wading around at low tide searching for sea anemone and orange and purple starfish. It had cliffs and crashing waves and seemed like the appropriate place to do something utterly unoriginal, like lose my virginity in the backseat of some guy's dinged-up, bright red BMW.

I didn't really know Paul but that didn't really matter. There we were, making sappy, sandy memories on the Malibu Shore, fifteen miles from home. It was nine p.m. on a school night. I needed to be back by ten.

"That was nice," he said, dragging a hand down the back of my head through my hair.

"Mm," I nodded, not really sure what to say back. I hadn't realized the moment was over, but there it was—our unceremonious end. "It's getting late, right?" I dragged my jeans over my lap. "Maybe you should take me home?"

"Yeah, absolutely," Paul shimmied backward, buttoning his pants. "I'll get you home." He wrinkled his nose, smiled, then swung his legs over the armrest and into the driver's side seat.

"Thanks," I said, trying my best to seem casual and upbeat, hiking my underwear and jeans back on, then creeping forward so we were seated side by side.

"You ready?" he asked, pinching an unlit cigarette between his bottom and top teeth.

"Sure thing." I buckled my seat belt and watched Paul run the head of a Zippo against the side seam on his pants, igniting a tiny flame. I turned my head toward the window and pressed my nose against the glass. There, in the not-so-far-off distance, an orange glow lit the sky, gleaming bright. *Brushfire.*

"Remind me, again?" He jangled his car keys.

"Hillside. Off Topanga Canyon."

"Right, sorry." He lit his cigarette and turned the ignition. "I'm shit with directions."

Chapter 2

Topanga was burning.

Helicopters swarmed overhead dumping water and red glop all over fiery shrubs and mulch. The air tasted sour and chalky and my eyes and throat burned from the blaze. Flaming hills, thick smoke—this used to seriously freak me out. Now, though, I sort of liked it. My whole town tinted orange and smelling like barbecue and burnt pine needles.

I was standing in my driveway, Harry's leash wrapped twice around my wrist. We watched the smoke rise and billow behind my house and I thought: *This is what nuclear war must look like. Mushroom clouds and raining ash*. I bent down, kissed Harry's dry nose, and scratched hard behind his ears. "One quick walk," I said. "Just down the hill and back."

He barked.

We sped through the canyon. Past tree swings and chopped wood and old RVs parked on lawns. Past the plank bridge that crosses the dried-out ravine, the Topanga Christian Fellowship with its peeling blue and white sign, the Christian Science Church, the Topanga Equestrian Center with the horses on the hill and the fancy veggie restaurant down below in their shadow. That day, the horses were indoors, shielded from the muddy, smoky air. Harry and I U-turned at the little hippie gift shop attached to the fancy veggie restaurant, and started back up the hill to my house.

Barely anyone was out on the road. It was dusky out, almost dark, so we ran the rest of the way home. I let Harry off his leash once we'd reached my driveway, then followed him around back to The Shack.

"Knock, knock," I said, rattling the flimsy tin door and pushing my way in. Nils was lying on his side reading an old issue of *National Geographic*. I kicked off my sneakers and dropped Harry's leash on the ground, flinging myself down next to Nils and onto the open futon.

"Anything good?" I asked, grabbing the magazine from between his fingertips.

"Fruit bats," he said, grabbing it back.

I shivered and rolled sideways, butting my head against his back.

"You cold?" he asked.

"No," I said. "Just a chill . . ."

He rolled over and looked at me. My eyes settled on his nose: long and straight and reassuring. "You freaked about the fire?" he asked.

I shrugged.

"They've got it all pretty much contained, you know. 'Least last time I checked."

I grabbed a pillow off the floor and used it to prop up my head. Harry was sniffing around at my toes, licking and nibbling at my pinkie nail. I laughed.

"What?" said Nils. "What's so funny?"

"Just Harry." I shook my head.

"No, come on, what?"

I grabbed his magazine back. "Fruit bats," I squealed, holding open the page with the fuzzy flying rodents. "I want one, okay? This year, for my birthday."

"Sure thing, princess." He moved closer to me, curling his legs to his chest. "Anything you say."

Nils is my oldest friend. My next-door neighbor. This shack has been ours since we were ten. It was my dad's toolshed for about forty-five minutes—before Nils and I met, and took over. The Shack is its new name, given a ways back on my sixteenth birthday. Years ten through fifteen, we called it Clubhouse. Nils thought The Shack sounded much more grown up. I agree. The Shack has edge.

"Have you done all your reading for Kiminski's quiz tomorrow?"

"No" I said, flipping the page.

"Where were you last night, anyway? I came by but Jeff said you were out."

Jeff is my dad, FYI. "I just went down to the beach for a bit."

"Alone?" Nils asked.

"Yeah, alone," I lied, dropping Nils's magazine and flipping onto my side.

Nils didn't need to know about Paul Bennett or any other boy in my life. Nils had, at that point, roughly five new girlfriends each week. I'd stopped asking questions.

"Hols, should we study?"

"Put on Jethro Tull for two secs. We can study in a bit." The weeks prior to this Nils and I had spent sorting through my mother's entire music collection, organizing all her old records, tapes, and CDs into categories on a shelf Jeff had built for The Shack.

"This song sucks," shouted Nils over the first few bars of "Aqualung." I raised one hand high in the air, rocking along while scanning her collection for other tapes we might like.

"Hols?"

"Yeah?"

"Your mom had shit taste in music."

I squinted. "You *so* know you love it. Admit it. You *love* Jethro Tull."

"I do. I love Jethro Tull." He was looking at me. His eyes looked kind of misty. *Don't say it, Nils, please don't say it.* "I miss your mom." He said it.

I sat up. "Buck up, little boy. She's watching us from a happy little cloud in the sky, okay?"

He tugged at my hair. "How come you never get sad, Holly? I think it's weird you don't ever get sad."

"I *do* get sad." I stood, dusting some dirt off my butt. "Just because you don't see it doesn't mean it isn't there."

Chapter 3

School.

7:44 a.m. and I was rushing down the hall toward World History with my coffee sloshing everywhere and one lock of sopping wet hair whipping me in the face. I got one "Hey," and two or three half-smiles from passersby right before sliding into my seat just as the bell went *ding ding ding*.

Ms. Stein was set to go with her number two pencil, counting heads, ". . . sixteen, seventeen . . . who's missing? Saskia? You here? Has anyone seen Saskia?" As if on cue, Saskia Van Wyck came racing through the door, *clickity-clack* in her shiny black flats, plopping down in the empty seat to my left. "I'm here, sorry! I'm right here," she said, dragging the back of her hand dramatically across her brow. *Adorable.* I slurped my coffee.

"Take out your books, people. Let's read until eight fifteen, then we'll discuss chapters nine and ten. 'Kay?"

I pulled my book from my bag and glanced to my left.

Saskia Van Wyck. Paul Bennett's girlfriend-slash-ex-girlfriend. I barely knew her. I only knew that she was skinny, pretty, marginally popular, and lived in this old adobe house just off the PCH, wedged right in between my favorite Del Taco and the old crappy gas station on Valley View Drive. I'd been there once, in sixth grade, for a birthday party, where no more than four kids showed up, but I remembered things: her turquoise blue bedroom walls. An avocado tree. A naked Barbie and a stuffed brown bear she kept hidden under her twin wrought-iron bed.

Saskia leaned toward me. "Do you have a highlighter or a pen or something I could borrow?"

"Yeah, okay." I reached into the front pocket of my backpack and pulled out a mechanical pencil. "How's this?" Suddenly I had a flash of that chart they show you in tenth-grade Sex Ed—How STDs Spread: *Billy sleeps with Kim who sleeps with Bobby who does it to Saskia who really gives it to Paul who sleeps with Holly, which makes Holly a big whore-y ho-bag who's slept with the entire school.*

"That's great," said Saskia, smiling. "Thanks."

I nodded and smiled back.

• • •

"Holly, move downstage a bit—to your left. And try your line again."

"Once more, with feeling," I deadpanned, closing my eyes and letting my head fall forward. *Gosh, I'm so clever.*

I walked downstage and shuffled sideways. "Wait—from where?"

"Start with: 'O, the more angel she, / And you the blacker devil!' And Desdemona, stay down—you're dead, remember?" Desdemona, or Rachel Bicks, who'd been sitting Indian-style on the stage sucking a Tootsie Pop, rolled her eyes and slinked back down. "Look more dead," Mr. Ballanoff barked. "Okay. Emilia, Othello. Go."

"'O, the more angel she, / And you the blacker devil!'"

"There's the spirit." Ballanoff turned toward Pete Kennedy, my scene partner, who was standing stage right holding a pillow. "Othello?"

Pete did his thing, kicking around the stage like an over-zealous mummy—he was big into *gesturing* and, somehow, still, he seemed so stiff. I *blah-blahed* back, just trying to keep my words straight without flubbing my lines. I don't think we'd made it through half the scene before Ballanoff was waving his clipboard, recklessly, *suddenly*, interjecting, "God, both of you, stop, please." Then, "Holly, god, come'ere."

I walked forward. "What? What's wrong now?"

"Where's the *fire*? He's just killed someone you love, he's calling her a whore—*where's the fire*, Holly?"

I shifted back and forth from leg to leg. "I ate too much at lunch. I'm tired. We only have three more minutes of class left. . . ."

He mashed his lips together, exhaling loudly, out his nose.

Ballanoff is Jeff's age about, early forties, but I've always thought he looked older than my dad until this year when Jeff aged ten years in a blink; going from salt and pepper to stark white in three months.

"All of you," Ballanoff shouted, "Learn your lines this week. Please. Work on feeling something *other* than apathy. Next class I expect changes." He smiled then, his eyes crinkling. "You can go."

I snatched my knapsack off the auditorium floor and lunged for the door.

"Holly."

"Yes?" I whipped around.

"Help me carry this stuff, will you?"

I trudged back down the aisle, grabbing a stack of books off a chair. Ballanoff took the other stack and together we walked out the theater doors, toward his office.

"How's your dad?" he asked, balancing his papers and books between his hands and chin.

"Fine. The same."

Ballanoff knew my mom in high school. They once sang a duet together from *Brigadoon*.

"How's Nancy?" I asked. Ballanoff's wife.

"Good, thanks." He unlocked his office door, kicked an empty cardboard box halfway across the room, then dumped the pile of books onto his cluttered desk.

I set my stack down on the floor next to the door. All four corners of his office were crammed with crooked piles of books, plays, and wrinkled papers. A tiny, blue recycling bin shoved against the wall was filled to its brim with empty diet Snapple bottles.

Ballanoff sighed, walked over to the mini fridge, and took out an iced tea. "I expect more from you."

"Yeah, I know."

"It wouldn't kill you to get a little angry, or to feel something real for a change." He paused for a bit, then said, "How are you, anyways?"

"Dreamy."

"That good, huh?" He collapsed into his black pleather desk chair, swiveling from side to side.

"Oh, yeah. Pep rallies and bonfires galore. Senior year really lives up to the fantasy."

He laughed, which made me happy, momentarily. "What about you?" I asked.

"What about me?"

"You know. How's life in the teachers' lounge?"

"Oh, hey." He took a long pull off his diet iced tea. "Same old shit, year after year."

I flashed my teeth. "I love it when you swear."

"I should watch it, right? Before Harper finds out and fires me for teaching curse words alongside *Othello*." Harper. Our principal.

"It's true. Look out. You're a danger, Mr. B."

"I should hope so." He slid two fingers over the lip of his wood desk. "Thanks for your help, Holly."

I perssed the sole of my sneaker against his shiny orange door. "Anytime."

"Tell Jeff hi for me, okay?"

"Will do." I pushed backward then, out of his office and back down the hall.

"Jesus, Nils, watch the windows."

Nils was all over some dumb girl, backing her into my driver-side car door, his grubby little fingertips pressed against the glass.

"Oh. Hi Hols, hey."

"Hi. *Move*, please."

He and the girl pushed sideways so I could get my key in the lock. "Much obliged."

The girl giggled and turned toward me. *Oh, no. Not her.*

"Hey, Hols? You know Nora . . ." Nora Bittenbender. From my Calc class. Before Nils she'd supposedly slept with two teachers: David Epstein and Rick Hyde. Pretty girl but *way* bland for my taste. Fair and freckled with these jiggly, big pale boobs she was always jamming into push-up bras and too-tight tank tops. Her weight fluctuated nonstop—skinny one week, chubs the next—and her taste, Jesus, *seriously questionable*. School ensembles that bounced between cheesy night-club clothes and oversized, heather-gray sweats. *Sexy.*

"Do you want a ride or not?" The hood of my car was covered in ash. I slid a finger through the dusty gray soot, then hopped inside. "I promised Jeff I'd take Harry out for a run after school, so either get in or I'm leaving."

"Right, yes! Okay." Nils ran over to the passenger-side door. Nora trailed him, holding on to the back of his shirt. "But could you drop Nora off on the way? She lives right by us, on Pawnee Lane."

No. "That's fine," I said. "Get in."

Nils crept into the backseat. Nora took shotgun. "Holly, thanks," she said. "I missed my bus."

"Yup."

"We have gym together, don't we?"

"Calc," I said, flooring the accelerator and, three seconds into my drive, nearly crashing into pedestrian Paul Bennett. *Good one, Holly.* I pulled to a stop and rolled down my window.

"Crap." He looked really great. He was wearing this old, thin, button-down with a small tear at the collar. His bangs lay on a diagonal across his forehead, hitting his eyes just so. "You missed me by a millimeter!"

"I'm sorry! I'm *so* sorry! Are you okay?"

Paul started toward my window, then, spotting Nils and Nora, stopped short and readjusted his backpack. "I'm fine. Just"—he waved his hands in the air and smiled—"startled, is all."

"Right. Sorry."

I watched his hair blow backward as he turned and walked on toward his car. Then I lightly pushed down on the gas and rolled out onto the main road.

"I didn't even know you knew Paul Bennett." Nils had scooched forward in his seat so that his face was floating somewhere over my armrest.

"I don't, not really."

"You sure? 'Cause he seems to know you."

I felt something un-nameable tickle my gut. Regret? Longing? I shook my head. "I mean, we have a class together. He knows my name, I guess."

"Maybe he likes you," said Nora, poking me in the shoulder.

Nils scoffed. "No offense, but, I don't think Holly's really Paul Bennett's type."

"What's that supposed to mean?" I turned sideways and gave Nils the icy eyeball. "What's Paul Bennett's type? Please! Pray tell."

Nils folded a stick of cinnamon gum into his mouth. "You know, blond. Willowy. WASPy. The anti-Holly."

"Saskia Van Wyck," said Nora, nodding.

I rolled my eyes. "Of course. Saskia Van Wyck, the anti-Holly."

"That's a good thing, Hols. She's plain spaghetti." He looked at me lovingly. "No sauce."

Nora twisted around in her seat so that she was facing Nils. "Can I have a piece of that?" She was biting Nils on the neck and pulling on his pack of gum. "I *love* cinnamon. I do."

We spent the next twenty minutes stuck in traffic on the PCH. In my rearview I watched Nils make eyes at Nora. *He's better looking than her, smarter than her, he's just better,* I thought. They were mismatched. Like fast food and fancy silverware. Or spray cheese and sprouted bread.

"Oh, hey! This is me. I'm up here, on the left," she said, "the green one with the tree." There was a porta potty parked on her front lawn next to a tall stack of aluminum siding. "We're expanding the kitchen. And adding a half-bath."

I turned up her steep driveway and stopped ten feet short of the garage. She kissed Nils on the mouth. *Smooch, smooch.*

"Thanks again, Holly." And then, to Nils, "Call me."

"Will do."

She was gone.

I kicked the car into reverse and started backing up. "Okay, get up here. I am not your chauffeur." Nils scooched from back to front, contorting to get through the tiny space between seats. We were side by side now. Neither one of us talking. I drove quickly back down Nora's twisty street and out onto the main road, where we passed my favorite rock. White and long and crater-faced; like a slice of the moon.

"Okay. What the hell, Nils, *Nora Bittenbender?*"

"So cute."

"Of course. *Cute.* What beats cute?" I snipped.

"Boobs."

"Right . . . of course. *Boobs* beats cute." I glared at him sideways. He had his head turned and tilted back, his hand hanging languidly out the window.

"You don't even know the girl, Holly."

This thing with Nils and girls started junior year with Keri Blumenthal, a pool party, and a stupid green bikini. Then before I could blink, my friend was gone and in his place was this dumb dude who *loved* Keri Blumenthal and lame bikinis and even though I'm *loath* to admit it, this is when things really changed for us. Keri Blumenthal wedged a wall between us. Fourteen days they lasted and still, when they went bust, that dumb wall stayed intact. "She talks like a baby," I said.

"Holly."

"And why does she wear those clothes?"

"Comfort . . . social conventions . . ."

"Not *any* clothes, pervert. Those *particular* clothes."

"Holly. Come on."

"Seriously, what's the deal with her and Epstein? Is that for reals, or no?"

"I dunno . . ."

"I just don't understand why you like her. You're better than—"

"Holly." He sat up really quick and grabbed my hand. "Stop it. Okay?" He tightened his grip and creepy tingles rolled up my arm. "I'm not gonna marry the girl."

I looked back at the road, mimicking Nora's babyish lilt. "You're not?"

Nils dropped my hand. "You're a weirdo, Holly."

I pursed my lips. "At least I'm not a baby with . . . big boobies."

"Weirdo."

I slapped him hard on the arm and turned up my driveway. We both laughed.

I parted ways with Nils and beelined for the fridge. Harry was at my heels begging for food, so I unwrapped a single slice of American-flavored soy cheese, rolled half into a little ball, and dropped the other half on the floor. He inhaled the thing in two seconds flat, not even stopping to chew.

I walked to my bedroom, simultaneously nibbling on my little ball of fake cheese and taking off my clothes, item by item. I slipped on my running shorts and a tank, grabbed Harry's leash, and poked my head into Jeff and Mom's room on my way to the back door. She'd been gone six months and somehow, the entire place still smelled like her: rose oil and castile soap. I don't know how that happens, someone dies and their scent stays behind. Jeff hadn't changed a thing. All her clothes were still on their racks in the closet, her perfume on the vanity, her face creams and make up in the little bathroom off their bedroom. Most days it was easy to pretend she was still around. Out at the store. On a walk. In the garden. Out with Jeff.

So I took the dog out running. Up the canyon, past Ms. Penn's place with that wicker chair she has tied to a rope so it hangs from her tree like a swing; up Pawnee Lane, past Nora Bittenbender's, past Red Rock Road, and out into town. I bought a ginger ale at the Nature Mart and walked back most of the way, trying to keep twigs and rocks out of Harry's mouth.

Later that night, around seven, Jeff came home.

"Hi, Dollface." He kissed my forehead and took a bottle of seltzer out of the fridge. He held it to his neck, then took a long swig, settling into his favorite wooden chair. "What's for dinner?"

"Tacos, maybe? I was thinking I'd drive down to Pepe's. Another night of pasta, I just might hurl."

Jeff laughed his sad little Jeff laugh and kicked off his

loafers. "'Kay, sounds good to me, whatever you want." Then he handed me a twenty. I put Harry in the car because he loves hanging his head out the window at night while I drive, and we sped down the hill, to the beach, to Pepe's, where I bought eight tacos: four potato, two fried fish, two chicken. I kept the warm white bag in my lap on the drive back, away from Harry, and thought about Mom for a second or two. Specifically, her hair: long and thick and dark, like mine. I sang along to a song on the radio I didn't really know the words to, and when my cell rang, I checked the caller ID but I didn't pick up. I didn't recognize the number.

Jeff and I ate in front of the TV that night, watching some cheesy dating reality show that he loves and I hate, but I humor him because he's my dad and his wife is dead and anything that makes him happy now, I'm into. So we finished dinner, I kissed him good night, and then I went out back to The Shack with my cell to listen to the message from my mystery caller. "Hi, Holly," said the voice on my voice mail, "it's Paul. Bennett. I'm just calling to see what you're up to tonight. Gimme a ring." *Click.* My heart shot up to my throat. We'd never talked on the phone. In fact, we'd never really talked.

I held the phone to my chest and considered calling back, I did, but the whole sex-in-his-car-at-the-beach thing had really struck me as a one-time deal. I called Nils instead.

"Hello?"

"It's me."

"You out back?"

"Yeah. Jeff's asleep in front of the TV and I'm bored."

"Be right there. I'm bringing CDs, though, okay?"

"Whatever you say." I flipped my phone shut.

"Holly-hard-to-get. Hi."

Paul and I were standing shoulder to shoulder outside my Chem class. He was wearing a battered old pair of khaki cut-offs, black aviators, and a brash grin. "You don't return phone calls?"

I stared at him, mystified, as he shuffled backward. I shook my head.

"Too bad." He blinked. "What do you have now, Chem?"

"Mm," I managed.

"You stoked?"

"What for?"

"Class." He cocked his head sideways, scanning my face for signs of humor, no doubt. "I'm kidding."

I looked at him blankly. Why were we standing there, talking still?

"Holly?"

"Hmm?"

"Are you okay?"

"I'm fine, yeah. Tired, I guess."

"Well . . . are you busy later?"

I nodded *yes I'm busy, sorry, can't hang out* and watched,

rapt, as he swung his pretty head from side to side. "I don't get you," he said.

I hugged the door frame as a couple of kids tried squeezing past me. "What's to get?" I asked, because seriously, *what's to get?* I was baffled, *really* perplexed by his sudden and obsessive interest in me. I wore ratty Levi's and dirty Chuck Taylors to school every day. I rarely brushed my hair. I had *one* friend besides my dog, and spent nights with my checked-out dad in front of the TV. What about me could possibly hold Paul's interest?

He flashed me one last look, gliding a hand along the wall, then disappearing into a crowd of kids in flip-flops and jean shorts standing around in a big square pack.

Was this some big joke or was I suddenly irresistible? Did I even *like* Paul? Did Paul truly like me? I peeled myself away from the door frame, turned a quick pivot, and shuffled into class.

Nils had his elbows pressed against the black Formica desktop and was fidgeting with some metal contraption with a long, skinny rod. I dropped my books down next to him. "What's that?"

"It's a Bunsen burner." Nils considered me. "What's wrong with you?" He moved sideways, making room. "You look pinched."

I grabbed a stool, dropped my bag to the floor, and plopped down next to him. "Just, no. Just—" I ran a finger over a crooked little heart that had been etched into the side of the desk. "Why Nora? Like, why go after her? Do you like her even?"

"Yeah, sure thing."

"No but, do you *like her* like her?"

"I like her enough." *Ick.* This sort of thing was classic *New Nils*-speak. Nils *post* Keri Blumenthal. Yes, maybe he'd had some experience this past year, and yeah, maybe I hadn't even gone past kissing with anyone pre-Paul . . . *still,* that didn't give Nils the right to be cagey and smug when I needed real, straightforward answers.

"What does that mean?"

Nils looked at me. He shrugged. "She's a nice way to pass the time."

I flinched. "Oh. Duh, of course." Then I opened my Chem book to the dog-eared page and pretended to read. So that was it. Sex. A way for Paul Bennett to pass the time. *Holly-pass-time. Holly-ho-bag.* I pressed my forehead to the crease in my textbook.

"What're you doing?"

"Resting."

"What do you care about Nora Bittenbender, anyway?"

"I don't."

"You sure you're okay?"

I sat up. "I'm fine." I gestured toward the Bunsen burner. "Come on. What the hell are we doing with this thing, anyway?"

"We're making s'mores," said Nils, pulling a misshapen Hershey's Kiss from his pocket and a crushed packet of saltines off the neighboring desk.

"Gross," I said, smiling for real this time, feeling a smidge better. "Just gross."

Chapter 4

Alone after school, I meandered through the canyon replaying my conversation with Paul from earlier, trying to decode our exchange as if it were a riddle or an exercise from my Spanish workbook. *I don't get you. I don't get you.* I ran the sentence on a loop in my brain, hoping I'd hear some hidden clue in Paul's inflection or phrasing. But no, no clue. In all my obsessing, I'd only succeeded in making myself dizzy and agitated. So I tried refocusing my energy. I took a breath, held it, and sprinted down the hill to the Old Topanga intersection, where I found myself stopped not ten yards off from that tiny hippie gift shop.

I went inside.

"Hi there."

"Hi," I said.

There, across the room, sat this new-agey lady, reading a book behind the register. "Can I help you find something?"

"Oh, I'm just looking. Thanks."

I zigzagged to the other side of the shop, past a creepy trinket display, complete with ceramic gnomes, scented oils, and cruelty-free, color-free lip gloss. I stopped to linger by the books.

The new-agey lady wandered over. "Looking for anything specific?"

I turned back to the bookshelf to survey the selection: electromagnetic therapy, transcendental meditation, mediumship. Then, a thought: Mom on a cloud with a megaphone, waving enthusiastically. "Do you have any books on, like, the afterlife or life after death or . . . ?"

She bent down beneath me and picked a book of the shelf.

"*Visitations*," I read out loud.

"Mm. That one really put everything into perspective for me. Wild." She was round, the shopkeeper lady. She wore a flowy, floor-length skirt and a button-down linen top she kept tied at her waist. Her earrings were miniature teakettles.

"Thanks." I flashed a polite smile and flipped through the first few pages.

The lady took another step toward me. "Looking for answers?"

"Oh, I don't know."

"Did you recently lose someone you love?"

"No."

She smiled and scrunched up her eyes. "I have a friend. Wait here."

She shuffled back to the cash register, picked a small tin off the countertop, and pulled a business card from beneath the lid. She was back before I could blink. "A friend of mine is a medium. Really terrific. My sister passed not too long ago and he was able to make a connection. Blew my mind."

"Wow. That's . . . yeah, that's great." I felt massively queasy. Mom loved this stuff: psychics, auras, white light, and positive thought.

"Here." She thrust the card into my line of vision.

"Oh, I don't—" I threw my hand up and waved it around. "I don't need that. Thanks, though."

"No, no, you *do*. Here." She took my hand, crumpling the card against my palm.

I'd had one previous reading with a psychic. When I was fourteen, with a friend of my mother's who insisted I steer clear of cigarettes and booze and instead suggested I visualize a purple light enveloping my body, each morning before for school. "I'm going to have to come back for the book."

Shopkeeper lady waved her hand dismissively.

"I didn't bring my wallet."

"I can put the book aside for you."

"Thanks." I stuck the card in my back pocket and walked

toward the door. "I'll be back," I said. "I just . . . you know. Need money."

Shopkeeper lady nodded, dragging a hand across her round hip. "Enjoy the day. Give my friend a call!"

I waved and pushed my way outside, the shop chimes clinking together as the door swung shut behind me.

"Hollllllllly. The hammer, please. Now." Nils had a nail clenched between his teeth and was balancing on a small step stool.

"Here, sorry." I handed him the hammer and went back to my bucket of paint. We were redoing The Shack for fall. One orange accent wall. A wreath made out of thirteen brownish leaves I'd found in our garden. Some gold-colored Christmas lights that Nils was busy tacking to the wall-meets-ceiling seam.

"Okay, so remember that time you went to church?" I asked, pinning my bangs back with a bobby pin.

"No."

"Yes, you do. With your cousin what's-his-face. Who lives down in Cardiff?" Harry was curled in a big sleeping ball of slobber and fur on the futon. He let out a loud snore.

"Oh right, right. Yeah, I remember. But that was temple." He grinned at me, crossing his eyes.

"Well, whatever. What I'm asking is, do you feel like you left with answers?"

"What sort of answers?

"Like, to questions you may have had. About . . . life. And the universe. Or whatever." I mopped some sweat off my forehead with a rag. It was ridiculous out. Blindingly hot.

"Like life and the universe or whatever?"

I threw a sponge at Nils's kneecaps and missed. It landed on the ground next to Harry. "Yes, you douche bag. Don't make fun of me. This is serious."

"Okay. *Jesus.*" He checked to make sure his jeans were still dry. "*No,* then. I don't feel like I left with any answers. But I wasn't really looking for answers."

I ran the back of my hands quickly down the sides of both breasts. I was doing this more and more frequently now, absentmindedly checking for lumps whenever Mom sprung to mind.

Nils continued hammering, then stopped abruptly, turning to face me. "Are you looking for *answers*, Holly?"

I tried looking chipper. "Maybe?"

He got down off the stepladder and sat between Harry and me on the futon. "Holly . . . ?" He whispered my name as if it were a question, staring into me until finally, I broke, reaching into my pocket and pulling out the little card from the new-agey shopkeeper lady. I handed it to him.

"'Frank Gellar: Psychic Medium.' What's this?"

"This lady gave it to me. I just—what if she's out there and wanting me to contact her?"

"Who?"

"Look, just don't laugh, okay?"

Nils looked uneasy. I covered my face with my hands, then whispered, "my mom."

"What?"

He pulled my hands down away from my face. "I can't hear you."

"My mother." I bugged my eyes out of my head and waited for Nils to say something shitty. But he just suddenly looked all sad.

"Hols . . ." He touched my hand. I flicked him away.

"Don't *Hols* me. You wait till someone close to *you* dies, then you see what sorts of crazy things you start considering. What if *I* died? Huh? You wouldn't contact"—I grabbed the card off the futon and checked the name—"Frank Gellar, if there was a chance he could bring us together one last time?"

Nils relented. "If you died, Holly, I would probably call Frank Gellar, sure."

I softened. "I just mean, what if she's trying to contact me and we can't connect because I don't know what's important and what's not. Like, what if she's sending me signs and I'm missing them?"

"Holly."

"Nils."

The phone rang. Nils feigned surprise. "Maybe that's a sign right there!"

I punched him hard in the arm, then lunged for my cell. It was Paul. I sent the call to voice mail.

Nils got back up on his stepladder. "Who was that?"

"No one," I said, picking back up my paintbrush. "I expected more sensitivity from you."

He turned to face me. "I loved your mom, Holly, you know that. Doesn't mean I'm gonna support you giving a whole bunch of money to some quack who's just gonna exploit your loss and feed you a bunch of hippie bullshit." He got back down off the stepladder, coming up behind me and slipping his hands around my waist. "Seriously, Hols, anything you need to do to feel better about your mom, I'm here for you. I just think this guy sounds like a joke."

"We don't know anything about him, though."

"Holly."

"He could be totally legit." I turned around and faced Nils and his hands slipped from my waist back down to his sides. "It was just a thought," I said, trying to sound casual. "Forget I even mentioned it, okay?"

"Holly—"

"Forget about it, it's done. Go finish the lights."

Chapter 5

Before she got sick, about four years before she died, Mom and I took a trip to sunny San Diego to visit a friend of hers who lived with her new husband by the ocean. We left Jeff at home. We wore one-piece bathing suits and swam in the cold sea and ate Taco Bell, which she never would have let me eat had we been stuck home with our soy cheese/granola/salad-for-supper diets. Astrid, her friend, liked Taco Bell. She liked cigarettes and the beach and tan skin and young men. So for one whole day and night Mom and I lived like Astrid. We got pink in the sun and ate nonstop: Taco Bell and ice-cream bars and shaved cherry ice from a stand in the sand. At night we listened to Bob Marley and made chiles rellenos with black beans and our own tortilla chips that we fried in a shallow pan filled deep with boiled oil. Astrid's son Jason came by to help us cook. He looked about the same age as Astrid's husband. I was twelve and he was blond and tan and after dinner he danced me around the room to Van Morrison's "Warm Love."

Then we watched an old movie on a tiny television.

Astrid fell asleep midway through the movie but Jason stayed alert, watching my mother watch TV. His eyes would dart between the screen and her face and when the credits finally rolled, he stood up, grabbed my hand, and said, "Let's make you a bed."

He fetched sheets and an afghan from a cupboard in the hallway and fixed me a bed on the couch with three silky pillows from the orange loveseat that I liked. Mom and Astrid were now in the kitchen. I could hear the water running and the clanking of dishes and silverware.

I slipped under the covers and he pulled the sheets taut on either side of me. "How's that?" he asked.

"Good." I nodded and watched as he reached for the light switch.

"You okay? You want water or something?"

"No," I said, studying the long swoop of bleached hair that hung down across his forehead. He smelled like chlorine and cologne. "How old are you?" I asked.

"Twenty," he said.

"Do you have a girlfriend?'

"Why, you interested?"

I felt my cheeks blush hot. He winked at me and flipped the light switch on the wall. The room went dark.

"You know, you really look a lot like your mom," he said. My stomach went warm. I'd heard it from others before but seeing the way he looked at my mother, then hearing him say those words to me made me feel really great. "Thanks," I whispered, my eyes acclimating to the dark. I could see his outline now, shuffling back across the carpet toward the kitchen. He was backlit and beautiful looking and only ten yards from my makeshift bed. "One day," he said, lingering in the doorway, "one day I bet you'll be her spitting image." He moved a hand across his forehead then, sweeping his bangs and all that bleached, shaggy hair, to one side.

Chapter 6

Lunchtime.

Saskia was two tables over from me, thoughtlessly picking at a plate of french fries and salad, while the girl across from her, Sarah something-or-other, talked and waved her hands around, punctuating points in her story by jabbing Saskia in the shoulder with her finger.

I ate my avocado sandwich alone at my regular table. Nils had late lunch on Wednesdays, so once weekly I ate on my own. Bagged lunch and homework. Or bagged lunch and a book. This time it was bagged lunch, my Spanish workbook, and Saskia Van Wyck. I was obsessed. Suddenly. How could someone who spent years loving shiny, willowy, well-adjusted Saskia be even slightly interested in someone like me?

I tucked some of the fabric from my dress up under my

bra and it stayed there, stuck to my sweaty skin. The temperature hadn't dipped below ninety in four days. We were indoors with AC and still, I felt as if I couldn't escape the heat.

Somehow, impossibly, Saskia looked fresh as a buttercup. Cool and put together but more importantly, *dry*. I pulled my dress loose from underneath my boobs and straightened up. Certain my face was shiny and pink, I tucked my head down, skimming my worksheet and wondering why I felt so nauseated. When I looked back up, she was staring back. We caught eyes for a second or two, then she turned back to her friend.

Gym. I considered skipping but then didn't. My grades had been crap after a shitty last spring and an uninspired fall, and since college applications were due in less than three months, I figured an easy A in Phys Ed couldn't hurt. So I sucked it up and went. I changed into my stinky gym shirt and shorts in the toilet stall off the changing room and hauled myself out onto the crispy, beige-colored field where the grass felt like straw beneath my sneakers. I played forty-five minutes of soccer in ninety-two-degree heat with a bunch of blond girls who seemed equally unexcited by team sports, then I dragged my sweaty self off the field and back to the locker room, where I took a twenty-five-second ice-cold shower before slipping back into my dry dress and sneakers.

After that, I walked to my car. I was trying to get the hair off my neck, scooping it all up in one fist and twisting it into a rubber band, when suddenly, there was Paul right next to me, matching me step for step. He wasn't saying anything. I looked at him and he looked at me and then we just kept walking. So I stopped. I turned sideways and said, "Can I help you with something?" And he cracked his knuckles and said, "Come with me."

After forty-five minutes of soccer, I said yes to a hike. I told him I had to stop home and get Harry, so we picked up the dog and drove up the mountain to Red Rock Canyon. Harry hung his head out the window and I chewed at my nails and wiped sweat from my forehead and watched Paul while he drove. He smoked two cigarettes, sang the chorus to a song that was playing on the radio, and every now and then he'd lean toward me as if he were trying to brush against me or something but the armrest and the stick shift were getting in his way.

We parked. We got out of the car and walked for a while. We walked and we walked and we didn't really say much, we just got hot in the sun and breathed hard, eventually stopping to sit on a rock.

Paul said, "I'm kind of obsessed with you, Holly."

I didn't know what to say back. I couldn't imagine anyone really, really liking me. "You're a liar," I said.

"I'm not." He put his hand in front of his face to block out the sun. "Remember when your mom died?"

"No," I said.

It took him a long minute before he got the joke but then he laughed so hard his eyes disappeared. "You're funny," he said.

"You think?" I pulled on my dress, now stuck to my skin. I was wearing an old gauzy cotton dress of Mom's and it occurred to me, suddenly, that I might be able to catch cancer through her clothes. I shifted around, then ran a hand discreetly down the side of my boob. No lumps.

"How come you seemed so fine afterward?"

I shrugged. They'd made such a spectacle at school when Mom died. They'd made an announcement over the PA system and I got tons of cards from teachers and even a few from students I'd never talked to. "I don't know," I said, which was the truth. I didn't know. I'd been so sick before she died. I'd lost weight with her, couldn't sleep like her, felt nauseated when her stomach hurt . . . I cried *all the time*. And then she was gone and all my sick feelings went with her. Charred up. Burned alongside her in the cremation oven.

I stared at him and he looked back at me and I wondered why he cared so much. I thought about that night at the beach. I pictured his mouth on my mouth and wondered if we would ever kiss like that again. If it would be better than it was before. I pictured his hands up my shirt, then his hands down my pants and wondered what it was, exactly, that he saw in me.

"Is that guy Nils your boyfriend?" he asked. He was tugging on a dead weed.

I said, "No."

"Do you want him to be?"

"No," I said again.

Paul looked at me for a long moment. "I think you're really special, Holly."

"Do you?" I asked, exhilarated.

He picked up a twig and threw it a few yards off. Then we got up and walked back to the car. Harry ran ahead, kicking up dust along the way. Paul kept behind me as we navigated past tangled roots, loose rocks, and the occasional pile of dog shit.

He never even tried to touch me.

When Harry and I got home it was just before six. Jeff's car was in the driveway.

"Helloooooo!" I hollered, coming up the steps. I kicked off my shoes and dropped my book bag, my gym bag, and Harry's leash on the chair by the door. "Anyone home?"

"We're in here," came Jeff's voice, which I followed into the kitchen. There he sat with Nils, two bottles of Pacifico and a deck of cards between them.

"What's this?" I picked up Nils's beer and took a sip.

"Gin rummy," said Nils.

"And underage drinking."

"He only gets one," Jeff countered, smoothing his hair with the flat of his palm.

I bounced across the tiled floor toward the fridge. "What's for dinner?"

"There's some salmon in there. And there's leftover squash from last night."

"Yum," I said, fishing through the vegetable drawer for a few stray zucchini.

"You're in a chipper mood," said Nils. "Where were you, anyway?"

"Hiking. With Harry." I took out the fish and a cutting board and set the oven to broil.

"Are you crazy? You went hiking? How could you hike in this heat?"

"I like it," I lied, pulling a wad of drenched, bunched dress-sleeve loose from under my armpit. Holding an ice cube from the freezer to my neck. "Movie night?" I asked, changing the subject.

"Again?"

"Again, yes," I said, holding a green squash in the air gleefully.

After dinner, we drove to the video store and picked something dumb to watch, a romantic comedy with a wedding *and* an explosion, and that whole night was great and the weekend that followed was great too, not because anything really fantastic happened, just because I finally felt a little happy and my future seemed somewhat less dismal and there was a person out there somewhere in the world who really thought I was something special. *Maybe things are on the up-and-up,* I thought. *Maybe now I have something good to look forward to.*

By Monday I'd worked myself into a near delusional state of bliss. I was back at school, all but skipping and whistling, and there was Paul, down the hall, leaning against his locker. I waved but he didn't see me because there was this whole huge group of kids blocking his view/my view, so I pushed past them, rehearsing my hello over and over in my head. I'd say, "Hey you," real casual sounding like it was nothing, just, *hey you . . .* which seemed so unremarkable but was really, so very intimate.

But as I got closer I saw what I hadn't seen before. He was attached to something. A girl. A blond, skinny Saskia Van Wyck. He was backing her into his locker. Within seconds my eyes were blurry with tears, which, to be honest, was probably best. Blurry was better. I turned and ran outside to my car. For most of first block I just sat, stuck to my hot leather seat, crying. I know it sounds so stupid because it's not like Paul was my boyfriend or anything, to be honest I wasn't even sure I really *liked* him; but something inside me said this was *it* for me: my life in turnaround. I'd paid my bad-luck dues with Mom back in May, and now it was time for something good. Or maybe luck doesn't work like that. Maybe I wasn't owed anything.

I didn't see Paul or Saskia for the rest of the day. On the ride home with Nils, I tried hiding my shit mood.

"What's wrong with you, weirdo? This morning you were bouncing off the walls, and now you look like you've been hit by a truck."

I didn't say anything.

He went on. "Classic bipolar behavior. Manic highs, awful lows . . ."

"I'm not bipolar, jerk-off." I punched him hard in the arm and then shifted the car into third. "I don't know what my problem is." That was true, I didn't.

He looked at me. He rubbed his arm where I'd hit him.

"Oh, please. That didn't hurt."

He pulled on his seat belt and twisted toward me. "Is there something you're not telling me?"

A wave of sadness rolled through my body. "Like what?" I tried looking less devastated. I missed the old Nils. The Nils I could tell *anything* to before his lame libido came along and wrecked everything. "My period," I blurted, figuring that would kill Nils's craving for a real heart-to-heart. "Don't sweat it. I'll be fine."

And I was. I pulled it together well enough to take Harry out for some exercise, to cook dinner for Jeff. We ate in front of the TV like we always did on Monday nights, but then afterward, when Nils called and asked if I wanted to meet up in The Shack, I said no. Enough for one day. I kissed sleeping Jeff on the cheek and locked myself away in my room. I listened to the crickets. I stared out the window. I shut all the lights off and lit a candle. I tried to read. I blew the candle out.

Then my phone rang. I grabbed it straight away, thinking it was Nils with one last push for The Shack. I didn't even check the caller ID. "What now?"

"Holly?"

It wasn't Nils. "Oh," I said. "It's you."

"Am I calling too late?" It was Paul.

"I was sleeping," I stammered. "I thought you were somebody else."

"Oh. No, it's me. Sorry to wake you."

I didn't say anything back. I wanted to make him feel bad.

He went on. "I just, I didn't see you in school today and I wanted to say hi."

"I saw *you*," I said.

He lit a cigarette. I could hear the flick of his Zippo, then one long, even exhale. I pictured the smoke shooting out of him in a skinny, gray straight line. "What's that?"

"With Saskia, I *saw* you," I huffed. He didn't say anything back, so I said, "So, what? Are you, like . . . back together with her or something?" I knew I had no right to be jealous. I must have sounded *insane*, but he was calling me and making me feel certain things and I felt deserving of an excuse or explanation.

"We are, yeah."

"Oh." That was all I could say, *Oh.* Not that him pressing

his body against hers in the hallway at school wasn't confirmation enough, but hearing him say it made it sound so officially . . . *official.*

"I like you so much, but Sass is going through a really hard time right now. Her brother's sick and she's really bad at handling family stuff and we've just known each other so long. I can't *not* be with her. She'd have a breakdown, I swear it." He paused, then said, "She's nothing like you, Holly."

"No kidding."

"No, I mean, she's not strong like you. She's breakable."

I couldn't imagine Saskia Van Wyck having a tough time with anything. I couldn't imagine her working up a sweat in gym, let alone crying over Paul or her sick brother.

I switched my phone to the other ear and put my head against the windowpane. "So, what, then, we're just friends?"

"Yeah. Yes, *please.* I would hate not being able to see you, Holly."

"Okay," I said softly, because it *was* okay. I wanted him, I thought—at the very least I wanted his attention—but the blond, willowy one had first dibs. What else could I do? I either said *good-bye forever* or I took second prize. Was that really such a bad bargain?

"You're the *best*," he said, really trying to sound sincere, I could tell. And I appreciated him saying it, I did, but Saskia was the best, not me. Saskia was number one, and everyone knew it.

Chapter 7

Our school cafeteria is fairly small. Forty or so big, round tables all crammed into this tiny indoor space encased in glass. We've got windows for walls mostly, except for the wall at the far end of the building where the kitchen and cashier are all set up. There's also a small patio with an additional ten tables or so, outside in the sun, but I've never sat there. I've sat at the same table since freshman year, the one that wobbles near the soda machine. The one with the clear view of Saskia Central.

"What's that?" Nora asked, pointing to my sandwich.

Another day, another lunch. This time with Nora, Nils's girlfriend or whatever the hell she was.

"It's a sandwich," I said, making *what-the-F* eyes at Nils.

"She means, what's *inside*, jerk-off."

"Avocado," I sang merrily, placating Nils. "And soy cheese."

Nils draped his arm around Nora. His fingertips grazed the top of her boob.

"So, I'm thinking of maybe having a costume party. For my birthday." Nora took a bite of lettuce and chewed while she talked.

"Oh, yeah?" said Nils.

"Mm. Or maybe I'll pick a theme? And people can dress to, like, fit the theme."

"Uh-huh."

"My parents okayed it. I mean, they'll be there, but they're cool, you know?"

"Yeah, yeah, sounds fun."

"Would you come, Holly? If I had a party?"

Saskia Van Wyck moved into my line of vision. "Ah, I think so. Which day is it?" She dropped her tray down next to that Sarah girl she's friends with, and let out a loud laugh.

"Not for a while. December fourteenth."

"Oh, right." I shot my attention back toward Nora. "What day is that?"

"It's a Friday," she said, and took another bite of lettuce.

I smiled, said *sure sounds great*, and turned back toward Saskia's table. She was laughing still. She looked happy, which for some reason made me really, really mad. She didn't look like a sad girl with a sick brother. She looked like a pageant girl who'd just been crowned queen.

"What're you looking at?" Nora asked, poking me in the shoulder.

"Ah, nothing." I said, watching intently as Paul made his way across the cafeteria. He dropped a plate of fries next to Saskia and touched the top of her head. They kissed. Quickly but with open mouths. I felt my chest tighten. I was sweating.

"You okay?" Nora asked.

"Yeah, what's up, crazypants, where are you today?"

"Nowhere." I stood up, infuriated. Paul was now sharing a seat with Saskia, absentmindedly dragging his fingers through her hair. "I gotta go."

"Where?" Nils asked. "We still have fifteen minutes till class starts. You aren't even done with your lunch."

"I know, I just, I have to study my lines for Ballanoff next block." I picked up my book bag and brown paper sack. "I'll see you later, at The Shack, maybe." I was off.

By the time I got to class, I was livid. Disproportionately mad. I huffed hello to Ballanoff, then we did our weirdo warm-ups. Alliterations, primal screaming, body shakes, and somersaults. Usually I'm too proud to partake. I skip this part of class, perched at the edge of the stage, watching the others and eating oranges left over from lunch. Ballanoff always lets me be, claiming it's fine so long as I realize he docks me points in participation. I'm good with that. Such a small price to pay in exchange for my pride.

That afternoon, though, I joined in. I yelled, I cried, I twirled around in dizzy circles. I sang "Peter Piper picked a peck of pickled peppers" ten times over, till I was breathless and tongue-tied. Then we broke off into groups. Me and Pete Kennedy, together again, same scene we'd been working on for weeks, the one we couldn't get right because I couldn't feel anything "genuine." This time, though, things were different. This time things were going *great*.

"O, the more angel she, / and you the blacker devil!"

Ballanoff made his way to our corner of the stage. He didn't interject or pull me aside or ask me where my "fire" was, he just watched as I wailed and screamed and clenched my hands into angry fists. Pete even did better. He was less mummy-like, which really made a difference. When we'd finished, Ballanoff clapped, one hand clacking against his clipboard. "Look at you two," he said. "Look at you, Holly, I don't think I've ever even seen you emote before. What *was* that?"

"That was me," I said. "Pissed off." I stood up, wiping a little bit of perspiration from under my chin. Then I grinned at Ballanoff and, feeling the first swell of exhilaration, hopped off the stage.

After school, on the walk to my car, I heard footsteps shuffling behind me, then a hand grabbed my arm. I turned around. "Oh." It was Paul. I shook my arm loose and kept walking.

"Whoa, whoa, whoa! Holly, come on, wait up." He quickened his pace so we were walking side by side. "What's happening?" he asked. "Did I do something wrong?"

"I don't want to talk to you," I said, not looking at him, taking my keys out of the front pocket of my backpack.

"Why? What could have possibly happened between last night and now? We're friends, remember?"

"We're not friends," I said, slowing as I reached my parked car. I lifted my keys and he grabbed for them, snatching them away before I could get my key in the lock.

"Give those back. Please," I pleaded.

"Tell me what I did and I'll let you have them back."

But it wasn't what he'd done. He hadn't *done* anything. I looked down at the pavement. There, to the left of my foot, was a smooshed lizard, half decomposed. Dead in the hot sun, looking serene. "It's not . . . you didn't *do* anything."

"Tell me why you're mad, then."

I didn't know why I was mad.

He extended his hand, letting my keys dangle from his pinkie finger.

I looked at him, then relented. "I just, I thought I could be your friend, but I can't. That's all." Then I slipped the key ring off his finger. He was bright red and the vein in his forehead had popped. He dropped both hands by his sides and took a step backward.

"Can I go now?" I asked, unlocking the door and getting in.

Paul shrugged and stood staring as I slammed my car door shut. I rolled down my window. "Please don't call me anymore," I said.

"Seriously, Holly? Why not?"

I pushed down hard on the gas.

Chapter 8

But he kept calling. Every half hour, my phone would ring and I'd send it straight to voice mail. He wasn't leaving messages, he just kept calling and calling. All throughout dinner it rang. "You sure you don't want to get that?" Jeff asked.

"I'm sure," I said, shoveling a forkful of pasta and cheese into my mouth.

"Well, would you mind turning it off, then? It's driving me crazy."

I got up from the table and turned off my phone, tossing it back into my book bag. Jeff and I continued to eat and not talk and then after dinner I went to my room. I thought about Paul and how much I hated him for making me feel so insignificant. I thought about Nils and Jeff and Harry and how they were all that I had. I thought about how next year I'd be leaving Topanga for god knows where, how I'd go to college then get married then have babies; how I'd get boring, get old, and then die. Or maybe I wouldn't get old. Maybe I'd die young like Mom. Dead at forty-two.

I dragged a shoebox out from under my bed. A handful of CDs, Mom's favorites, the ones I like keeping close to me. I pulled out a Neil Diamond disk and slipped it into my stereo. I skipped to track nine and lay back on my bed while my song played. "Holly Holy." Mom's song. *My* song, she'd said. I was named for it.

I listened to that on repeat for an hour or so, drifting in and out of sleep. Then, three raps came on my window. I sat up. I screamed. It was Paul.

"Shhhh. God. Holly, I'm sorry, I just wanted to see you and you weren't picking up your phone." He looked a little nutty. His hair was all mussed and sticking up.

"Are you insane?"

"No, just lemme in? Okay? Please?"

I checked the clock. Twelve fifteen a.m. I got up, tiptoed to the front door, and undid the dead bolt. I poked my head out the crack and called to the side of the house. "Over here," I whispered, and Paul came running.

"Take off your shoes," I said.

He slipped off his sneakers, placing them side by side on our front porch. Together we slid in our socks across the silky wood floors, back down the hall to my bedroom.

Inside, Neil Diamond was still playing my same song over and over. I shut the door behind us and sat down on my bed. "Well?" I said.

"I like your room."

"Thanks." I bit my top lip. "What do you want?"

"Is this Neil Young?"

"Neil Diamond," I corrected.

"Right. That's what I meant."

"Why are you here?"

He looked at me. "I just want to know what happened today."

"Nothing happened," I said softly, worried Jeff would hear. "I just don't want to be your friend anymore. I can't be your friend." I clenched my teeth shut and put my hand to my heart, trying to slow its insane pace.

"Why not?"

"I told you . . . ," I said, looking down. "You have enough friends already."

He pointed toward the bed. "Can I come over there?"

I shrugged.

"Is this about Saskia?" He was sitting next to me now. "I explained that to you."

"You were kissing her."

"When?"

"Today in the cafeteria."

"She's my girlfriend, Holly. I have to kiss her." But he

didn't have to kiss her. He didn't have to date her or love her or run his fingers through her hair. It's a choice, love. Even if she were threatening pills or razorblades, *blackmailing* him into loving her, the least he could do was look miserable loving her back.

"You looked happy," I said.

He slid closer to me, so our arms were touching. My stomach flipped and I moved sideways, away from him.

"You're tired," he said, suddenly seeming extraordinarily sympathetic.

I nodded. "You should go."

He stared back at me for a long second, then shrugged. "We could get into bed together?"

"What's that?"

"I promise not to do anything." He stood up then, pulling back my sheets. "We'll just sleep."

"How? *No.*" We wouldn't just sleep. We'd lie side by side awake and unhappy. If he touched me, I'd be unhappy. If he didn't touch me, I'd be unhappy.

"Come on, under the covers." He crept into bed, dragging the floral comforter up to his chin.

"I'm not getting into bed with you," I said. But he grabbed my hand and pulled me down. Not meaning to, I laughed. Then we were in bed together, under the covers, Neil Diamond singing "Holly Holy" over and over and even though he'd promised he wouldn't try anything, it only took about a minute before his hands were laced around my waist from behind. He pulled me into him. "Don't do that," I said.

His face was buried into the back of my neck. "Do what?" He took a breath. His hands slid up my shirt.

"That," I whispered, "don't do that." I turned onto my back. He kissed me. And it wasn't like last time, in the car. Last time felt wrong, but this time felt great. So funny, how something so wrong can feel so right. How before at the beach it all felt so empty, and how now, hating him and wanting him and feeling guilty about Saskia all rolled into one really wonderful feeling. He slipped my shirt over my head. "Can I stay here tonight, Holly?"

"You have to leave before Jeff gets up."

I could hear him sliding his pants off under the covers. "I think about you all the time," he said, and then he pulled me into him and I let him say sweet things to me, I let him slide off my underwear. "Is this okay?" he asked, running a hand across my stomach. I nodded and brushed my lips against his lips. I knew there was another person to consider. I knew he loved her and not me. But it was my life and my bed and I wanted to feel what I wanted to feel. *If I die tomorrow,* I thought, *at least I'll die knowing I felt something real.*

Chapter 9

So here's where things started to get a little mixed up.

I suddenly had a secret. And it made me feel guilty, yeah, but I also felt really fantastic. I felt the opposite of dead, really what I'd been striving for, and someone suddenly wanted me in a way I hadn't been wanted before. I didn't even mind having to keep things to myself. I mean, I thought the whole situation was really unfortunate, but I knew that I was the one he wanted more. That if she weren't so fragile, so unstable, he'd be with me for real. No Saskia. No secret affair.

"She's frigid."

"No, she's not."

"Holly, she is, she won't have sex with me."

We were in the back of my car, parked at the beach. Paul was smoking. My windows were rolled up.

"You're lying," I said.

"I'm not."

"You've been together *three years*. You've had sex with her." I buckled and unbuckled my seat belt.

He shook his head. "She's saving herself." He laughed and dragged off his cigarette. "So ridiculous, that we're still together . . ."

I hated hearing him say it: He was with her, not me. It had only been two weeks, the two of us doing what we were doing, and already I felt possessive.

He rolled onto his side and took my face between his hands. "It's so much better with you. It's easy. It feels right with you." I loved this. When he compared me to her. Things were easier with me. I was better than her.

The day before at school, I'd watched them in the hall together. Bumping hips while they walked. I'd watched her whisper something in his ear while he grabbed at her hands and bit the collar on her orange Lacoste polo. Three girls passed by, waving hello, and Paul leaned into Saskia and kissed her. He slipped her the tongue in front of everyone and she smiled, mid-kiss, and pushed him away, hitting him gently with the heel of her hand. Nils was with me. He was watching too. We leaned against our lockers in the hallway, sharing a bag of cheese popcorn. He said, "Those two make me want to puke. Seriously. Happiness like that should be outlawed."

And he could say what he wanted, but it all looked like lies to me. I felt bad for her. Fragile, frigid Saskia Van Wyck. *Poor little girl,* I thought, watching them stroll right past me. Their arms linked like paper dolls. *You think he's yours, but he's not,* I thought. *You think he's yours, but really he's mine.*

Chapter 10

Once, years ago, Mom hosted a crystal convention in our living room.

I was ten, padding around in socks and my long white nightgown while dozens of new-age hippies milled about sipping Kombucha tea, fondling rocks, and discussing *energy*.

"Who *are* these people?" Jeff asked. He was sitting on the granite island in the middle of our kitchen.

"I have no clue," I said, running toward him, scaling the side of the island so we could sit side by side.

"You think they know we live here?" Jeff asked. He was twirling a long, rose-quartz baton between his thumb and middle finger.

"No way," I said, getting settled, eyeing the crowd.

Mom moved easily from circle to circle, beaming, refilling

cups, stopping occasionally to check out a rock and discuss its unique shape and healing capabilities.

"I like *that* lady," I said, tilting my head toward a woman wearing a neon yellow jumper, inspecting a piece of amethyst. "I like her braids," I said, tugging on my own hair.

Jeff nodded. "Or what about this guy?" he said, pointing at this young dude with sandy hair hovering around my mother. "He's been trying to talk to Mom for the last half hour." Jeff looked at me. "You think he likes her?"

"Like, *likes* her?" I asked, horrified. "Ew. No."

"I think he *likes* her," Jeff said, amused. We both looked back at my mom. The guy was trying to edge his way into my mother's conversation with another woman.

"I'm right. You *know* I'm right," Jeff said, nudging my shoulder.

"Maybe." I nodded, turning to face him. "But doesn't that make you mad?"

He put a hand on my head. "It makes me *proud*," he said, happily mussing my hair, then pulling me forward and into a tight embrace.

Chapter 11

Nils was suddenly suspicious. He'd stopped dicking around with Nora Bittenbender long enough to notice my hysterical good cheer.

"You seem different," he said, folding down a page in his book and turning toward me.

I shrugged.

We were in The Shack, after school. It was almost six and dusky out.

"I just—I get the distinct impression that you're hiding something from me."

I turned onto my side, amused, and faced him on the futon. "Oh yeah? Like what? What am I hiding?"

"I dunno. You're happy all the time. Like, all of a sudden, things are great."

I forced a frown and brushed a stray hair off Nils's forehead. He looked at me for a beat. "Lemme guess: You're in love!"

I snorted.

"Or maybe you've just won the lottery!"

"Could be."

"Or maybe you got that adorable little fruit bat you've always wanted. The one we saw splashed across the glossy pages of *National Geographic* not too long ago. . . ."

"That very same one?" I played along excitedly.

"That very same bat."

I put my hands to my heart. Nils took a breath and dropped his head back down on the bed. "So what's the real deal?"

I flipped onto my back and fixed my eyes on the ceiling. I couldn't tell him about Paul. I just couldn't. "No deal. I'm putting on the Christmas lights. It's getting dark." I rolled to my side and stuck the plug in the socket.

"Holly."

"Nils."

"Come on, no kidding. What's up?"

"Nothing. I just feel good. There has to be a reason for that?" I tried my best to look believable. "Maybe the cloud has finally lifted."

"I thought we told each other everything."

"We don't tell each other everything."

"Yes, we do."

"No, we *don't*, loser. I don't know anything about you and your thing with that girl."

"That's because you don't *want* to know anything. I'd tell you if you asked. And why can't you say her name, Holly? You know her name."

"Yes, I know her name."

"Say it."

"Nora . . . Slut-bender."

Nils sat up, pissed. "She's not a slut. What, just because she's not some perfect little virgin, she's a slut?"

"Fiiiine, she's not a slut. I still don't like her. And you don't like her either! Remember? She's dumb, Nils. You're just with her 'cause she'll have sex with you."

"You're jealous."

I laughed. "Jealous of *what*? Her *constant* giggling? All that bottomless *depth*?" I got up on my knees. "Oh! Or! Watch for her birthday party costume. Bet you anything it involves a bikini!"

"Okay, Holly, enough."

I tilted my head to one side. "You're a smart guy, Nils. I don't understand why you'd go out with a girl like that."

"One day you'll get it. You'll invest more than two seconds in something or someone, then we'll talk."

"You think you know everything about me?" I stood up. "You don't know everything about me. I've *invested* in things you know nothing about."

"Clearly." We looked at each other. Nils grabbed my hand and dragged me back down. He looked me straight in the eye.

I wilted a little. "Look, I can't talk about it, okay? Just respect that, please? Because I can't. Not now, anyways."

"All right."

I grabbed him and wrapped my arms around his neck. Then held on tight for second or two before pulling back. "Do you bring her here?"

"Who? Nora?"

I nodded, my hands sliding to his shoulders. "Do you?"

"Holly, no. Come on. This is our place."

We linked pinkies. Then we both slid back down onto our backs with our books. Nils reached over and slipped a finger through my hair. "I love fighting with you," he whispered.

I dragged my knees to my chest. "Exciting, isn't it?"

"Makes me feel so alive!" he teased, pulling on a thick chunk of hair and jolting my head hard to one side.

Chapter 12

Mid-November. I was helping Ballanoff carry two huge stacks of books back to his office. We were talking about dumb stuff. Surface stuff. School and Dad and a new section from *The Crucible* we were working on in class. And then came a quick lull in the conversation and who knows why I said what I said but here's what came out when I opened my mouth: "Jeff says you had a crush on my mom."

It's true. Jeff claims Ballanoff was really into my mother in high school.

You should have seen his face. Frozen deer. Spotlights. Or headlights. Or whatever. "He says that, huh?"

I nodded. "Is it true?"

He fished his keys from his jacket pocket, then he undid the lock on the door. "Come on in. Stay a while." We both dropped our books onto his messy desk. "You want iced tea?" He bent down by the mini fridge.

"Sure."

"Diet?" he asked, grabbing two Snapples.

"Fine by me."

He tossed me my drink, then sat down across from me. "Yes. True. I had a crush on your mother."

"Really?"

"Really."

This was amazing to me. I loved the idea of my mother existing pre-Jeff. There'd only ever been one other guy I knew anything about, hairy Michael, Mom's college boyfriend. But now there was this, too. "Did you do anything about it?"

"Like what?"

"I dunno. Did you tell her? Did you *pursue* her?" He just looked at me, so I leaned forward and said, "Mr. B, did you *date* my mom?"

He half laughed/half coughed, as if he were clearing his throat. "No, Holly. I didn't date your mom."

"Did you ever kiss?"

"Holly."

"Come on, you're giving me nothing."

He shifted around in his seat, pursing his lips. "Once. When we were your age, about. It wasn't anything. I don't think she was really that into it, to be honest."

I blinked. "Were you sad when she died? I mean, I would have been so sad if someone I'd really liked once had died."

"Yeah, of course. I was very sad." And then he really looked it. I could be wrong, but I swear to god his eyes got a little wet.

"I want to go see a psychic," I blurted.

"What for?"

"You know. I wanna see if I can make a connection. Just so I know she's okay."

Ballanoff shifted around in his seat.

"Know any good mediums?" I joked, babbling on. "I got a card from this lady at the bookstore in town. That new-agey place right next to Nature Mart? She gave me the card of her friend." I paused a second and when Ballanoff didn't say anything, I said, "You think I'm crazy."

"I don't think you're crazy at all."

And then we stared at each other for a minute, which kind of freaked me out but I think Ballanoff just got really sad, suddenly. "You look so much like her," he said. Everyone says that. All the time people say that and I know it should make me feel really great but all it ever truly does is turn my gut. Same hair, same skin, same violin dimples on the small of my back. And if I look like her, who's to say I won't die like her?

"Heard it before. Dead ringer," I said, rolling a split lock of tangled hair between two fingers.

Chapter 13

Paul and I had figured out a system for seeing each other. Mainly school nights, after midnight. After Jeff and Nils and Saskia were asleep, he'd drive over and tap my window and I'd run down the hall and open the front door and then he'd crawl into bed with me.

"Ballanoff and my mom kissed once, when they were, like, seventeen." I slid my arm across Paul's waist.

"Shut up."

"It's true," I whispered. "He told me today. After class."

"Doesn't that creep you out?"

"I think it's nice. I like thinking about my mom when she was my age . . . like, I like the idea of her doing things before she was my mom or Jeff's wife. You know?"

Paul nodded and put a hand on my head. "Why do you call Jeff Jeff?"

"Sometimes I call him Dad to his face. But I dunno, when I was little I just thought it was really funny, calling Dad, "Jeff." I think I wanted to be grown up already. And it seemed like a very grown-up thing to do."

He moved his hand from my head, sliding it down so he was holding my hair. "What did you call your mom?"

I bent my head back so I could look at him. "Just Mom."

He laughed.

"Why's that funny?" I bit his shoulder and wrapped my leg around him under the covers. "I kinda can't wait for you to meet him."

"Who?"

"Jeff. Duh." I pressed my nose to his armpit. He smelled like a muted mix of Right Guard and BO.

"Holly," he said, getting up on his elbows to face me. "I can't meet Jeff."

"Why not?"

"Well, what're you gonna say, 'This is my friend Paul, he's not my boyfriend but we sleep together sometimes. Oh, also, he's got a girlfriend.'"

"Well, I wouldn't have to say any of that. I could just say you're my friend. That's the truth."

"Yeah but, what if he knows Saskia's parents or something?"

"Saskia's parents? He doesn't."

"You can't know that for sure. What if he does?"

I sat up. "So you're never gonna meet my dad? What about Nils? You know he's already started asking questions and I don't know how much longer I can hide this from him—"

"What do you mean, he's asking questions?"

"Well, you know, I think he's noticed how happy I am."

"If you tell anyone about us, I swear to god, Holly—"

"You swear to god *what*?" I pulled on the sheet, hiking it up under my arms the way naked women sometimes do on daytime soaps.

"I'm just saying, no one can know. They just—they *can't*." He lowered his voice a notch. "Saskia would die if she knew. We can't ever tell anyone."

"Well, what if you guys break up? We can't be together then? Like out in the open, for real?"

He softened. "If we break up, yeah, I guess then we can talk. But you can't tell anyone, Holly. You can't. No one can ever know about this, okay?"

I nodded, but I wanted to cry. Instead I sucked it up and lay back down and tried to remember why this whole thing felt so great to begin with.

He nuzzled up next to me then, resting his head on my chest. "I love being with you. I do."

"I know," I said, lacing my fingers through his fingers.

He went on. "It would be a real shame if somebody found out about us and all this had to stop."

My stomach churned. I flexed my fingers so that our hands were no longer entwined. He bit my earlobe and slid his free hand between my thighs. "Your hair smells so nice. Like roses."

"Different shampoo," I mumbled, rolling away from him and onto my side.

Chapter 14

As if on cosmic cue, the next day in World History, Saskia and I got stuck working together on this horrific group project—an Ancient Mesopotamia–themed collage.

"Do you have any clue what we're supposed to be doing?" She was staring at me, brushing her fingers over the tips of her hair.

"Not really," I said, giggling like a nervous twit. "Feels more like fourth grade arts and crafts." I stood up and circled around to the back of my desk.

"So we just, like, collect a bunch of images and paste them all together?"

We were pushing our desks together and all I could think was *this so isn't my fault but Paul's gonna kill me.* "Yeah, basically," I said. "I guess we can photocopy some stuff from the library. And there's stuff in our books we can use too."

Saskia plopped down in her seat. "I mean I know we know each other, so it seems stupid me introducing myself to you, but I don't think we've ever officially . . . *talked*. I'm Saskia."

"Holly." I said, checking the clock on the wall. *Crap, fifteen more minutes of this. Tick. Tock. Tick.*

"You went to my elementary, didn't you?"

"Same sixth-grade class."

"Ms. Shapiro?"

I nodded.

"Yeah, I totally remember."

Saskia leaned forward, lightly touching one of my dangly silver earrings. "I love these," she said. "Whenever you wear them I always stare. Have you noticed? I stare at people way too much."

"I hadn't noticed." I wished I had.

"Where'd you get them?"

"What?"

"Your earrings. In L.A.?"

"Oh. They were my mother's," I said. And then that kind of killed the conversation because she totally knew about my mom. Everyone knew. No one ever knows what to say.

We poked through our textbooks for the last ten minutes of class. I zoned out somewhere around page four hundred, rereading the same picture caption over and over, thinking about was how nice Saskia seemed, and about how Paul would freak if he ever found out about this—she and I paired up for class. Then I pictured Mom on her cloud. Then the bell rang and we pushed our desks back into place and Saskia turned toward me and said, "So, you wanna just bring a whole bunch of photos to class next time and I'll do the same and then we'll just start pasting stuff together?"

"Sounds like a plan, " I squeaked, grabbing my book bag and bolting for the exit.

"Hey, wait!" she yelled after me. "We didn't even divvy up the time line! Which half do you want?"

I was already out the door. "Whichever," I said, looking back over my shoulder. "I'll take invasion of Greece and everything after!"

"Okay!" she said, waving good-bye. And then that was it. Another secret to keep. Saskia Van Wyck: my brand-new best girl friend.

"Where to?"

Paul and I were driving into L.A. His idea. He said he was taking me somewhere great.

"It's not a place, exactly. I mean, it's a place, it's just not like, a *place* place."

We drove all the way up Sunset, away from the beach into the sticky city. We drove with the windows open and the music blaring and the air got hotter each mile we clocked on the odometer. We didn't talk much on the drive there, which was fine because I didn't really feel like talking, and then Paul finally stopped the car on this pretty little residential street somewhere in Hollywood.

"Where are we?"

"Hollywood and Sierra Bonita."

I looked at him, perplexed.

"It's haunted," he said. "Supposedly. I figure we could sit here for a little while, just to see."

"See what?"

"You know. Maybe if you concentrate really hard, you'll be able to, like, *feel* your mom. Or something."

And that's when I realized that this was the nicest thing anyone had ever done for me. I flung my arms around his neck and instantly wanted to cry but didn't, I just held on to him, letting him rub my back, and then I sank back in my seat and looked across the sky at the sun, which was setting. He slipped a hand around my neck and turned the car off.

I closed my eyes and I thought about Mom, but no more cloud fantasy. I thought about how she looked when she was still young and pretty, before the cancer had corroded her body. I pictured her healthy and perfect and then I said what I wanted to say to her from inside my head. I said, *I miss you Mom I love you Mom nothing's the same with you gone.* I told her about Jeff and how sad he'd been these past few months, how the closets were still packed with her clothes and how the house still really smelled like her. I told her about how Jeff had said even Harry had cried the morning she died. And then I talked about school and about Paul and I told her how guilty I felt *but isn't he great because he's brought me here. Maybe it's all worthwhile,* I thought, *because really he's brought me to you.*

And then I smelled smoke and looked to my left and Paul was smoking a cigarette, his feet kicked up on the dash, his eyes wide open staring out the window. And I said, "Hi. What're you looking at?" And he just turned and smiled at me and said he wasn't looking at anything.

"Did you feel something?" he asked. And I said I did and then I grabbed his hands and said thank you a million times over and then I told him about the medium I wanted to see. I told him about the lady in the new-age shop in Topanga and how I wanted to see if her friend could bring me a message from my mother. "Will you come with me?" I asked.

"You really want me there?" he said.

And I said yes, and he said, "I'd be honored."

And I just knew right then that what we were doing was really okay. That I wasn't a bad person and that as nice as Saskia seemed, that this thing with me and Paul was bigger than either of us had expected it to be. I thought, *Saskia's sweet but she'll have to step aside.* And then Paul started the car. He threw his half-smoked cigarette out the window and laid into the gas and then we were driving; back down Sunset, all of L.A. going dark in Paul's shiny rearview mirror.

Everything was really great after that. For twenty-four straight hours I walked around feeling super cheery and together. I went home, had dinner with Jeff, slept through the night, made a whole bunch of photocopies at the library before school the next morning . . . then managed to cut, paste, and distance myself from Saskia Van Wyck all through World History.

That night, Nils and I read next to each other in The Shack for about an hour or so. We picked at a plate of burnt brownies his mom had made—"reject brownies," she'd called them—and moved around a whole bunch trying to get comfortable on the futon with our novels.

After that I went back to the house. I crawled into bed. I waited for Paul.

Paul's visits were, for the most part, unplanned, but had become pretty predictable. Monday nights were always no good because of obligatory family crap and weekends were shit because weekends belonged to Saskia. So Tuesdays and Thursdays were gold, Wednesdays, too, but Wednesdays were wild cards and whether he showed up or not usually hinged on his mood. This was a Thursday, and since this had started Paul had never missed a Thursday. So I just sat in my bed and waited. I lay on the floor and waited. Time ticked by, the moon rose, I listened two and a half times over to a birthday mix Nils had made for me the year before, and then . . . nothing. It was one thirty a.m. I checked my phone. I looked out the window and checked the driveway. I tried to sleep but couldn't, and when I finally realized he wasn't going to show, I got Harry out of his stinky little bed on the kitchen floor and made him sleep with me.

The next morning I showered really quick and rushed to get to school early. I had twenty minutes before classes started. I sat on the hill by the parking lot and watched for Paul's BMW. At last, he showed, at twenty to eight, and I skipped down the hill toward his car.

"Hi," I said, looking around before leaning in for a kiss.

He pulled back, sinking his body back into the car. "What're you doing? Holly, seriously, get away."

I flinched, then quickly covered with a smile. "Why? No one can see us. What's the big deal?"

He grabbed his bag off the passenger side seat, stood up, and slammed his door shut. "Just, not at school, okay?"

I looked down. I mumbled, "Wouldn't want your precious Saskia to see . . ." Then, "Where were you last night, anyway?"

"I was at home."

"*Home* home?

"*What?* Speak English." We were walking now. Toward the side entrance by the gym.

"It was a Thursday."

"*English*, Holly."

"I just mean you could have called if you weren't going to come by. I waited up for you."

He stopped and turned toward me. "Holly. We didn't have plans. I didn't ask you to wait up."

"But you always come by on Thursdays."

"Holly." The way he kept saying my name over and over made me feel so totally small. "You're not my girlfriend." *You're not my girlfriend. You're not my girlfriend.* It echoed in my ear. *I hate you,* I thought as he dragged me across the taupe-colored field to the bleachers. We ducked underneath. "Do we need to set some ground rules?" It was cool now where we stood. Mostly shady save for a few skinny bars of gold light that fell across Paul's body and onto the dry lawn beneath our feet. "I like you, Holly. I do. But I'm not gonna do all this girlfriend-boyfriend bullshit with you, okay? I already have one relationship I have to manage." He pulled a pack of Camels from his pocket. "What we have should be easy."

"So *what?* What does that mean? I don't get to have *any* expectations?"

He lit a cigarette and with the filter pinched between his teeth he said, "Well, when you put it like that, you make me sound like a complete dick."

I glowered back.

"Don't look at me like that," he wheezed, taking a deep drag, then exhaling. "You knew what this was. You knew how this had to be. I'm not making you spend time with me, Holly. You want out, you say the word."

I looked down at the ground and kicked a pile of dirt.

He slid his pointer finger under my chin. "Why do you have to be so adorable?" he asked, lifting my face up, then pressing his lips to my lips. ". . . Needy little girl," he cooed. My stomach turned over. *I'm not needy,* I thought, pulling backward, slipping one hand around his head and grabbing on to this shaggy little chunk of hair he had hanging down the back of his neck. "That feels nice," he whispered, so I tightened my grip and yanked down. "Fuck, Holly. What the hell?" He let out a small cry, then grabbed my face real quick and kissed me so hard that it hurt.

"Ow, *Christ,*" I squealed, pulling back and stumbling sideways.

He laughed and shook his head, "You're a funny little girl, you know that, Holly?" He wiped his mouth dry on his shirtsleeve. "See you around," he said, sucking at the last of his cigarette and chucking it into a baked little patch of crud on the ground.

Chapter 15

I spent my open block fifth period sitting on the basketball court, folding and unfolding that psychic's business card. FRANK GELLAR: PSYCHIC MEDIUM. I read the words over and over again. Then I riffled around in my bag for my phone, which I found and fondled for one solid, excruciating minute before working up the nerve to finally dial.

"Hi, this is Frank . . ." *blah blah blah* . . . My call had gone straight to voice mail. "Leave a message and I'll get back to you as quickly as I can. Thanks and god bless." I'd expected a pretty pervy-sounding guy. For him to sound the way most new-age dudes around Topanga sound—super breathy and sexed out. Frank, though, just sounded old.

"Hi," I chirped in response to the mechanical beep. "My name is Holly Hirsh. I got your number from—" and then

I realized I didn't know the name of the woman I'd gotten his card from, so I said, "well, I got your number and was hoping to make an appointment to . . . well, I was hoping to make an appointment." I left my cell number before hanging up.

So Frank was old. I found this comforting. *Old Frank*, I thought, feeling triumphant. I'd called! I'd done something proactive! I'd taken a step in a direction that would lead me somewhere really terrific. Or enlightening. Or something.

In the car after school with Nils and Nora, I told them both what I'd done.

"Jesus, Holly. I thought we talked about this."

"So? You think every action I take has to be filtered through you? I can make my own decisions." I turned up Pawnee Lane. "It felt right."

"Oh, well . . . if it *feels* right."

Nora reached into the backseat and slapped Nils on the thigh. "Don't be a dick, I think it's great."

I glanced to my side. "You do?"

"Yeah. I love that guy on TV. What's his name? Who helps all those people talk to their dead family members? There was this one episode where this lady's son had killed himself and she was just really hysterical, like, crying and crying. But then her son came through in the reading and talked about this little private joke they'd had about Gruyère? You know, the cheese? And the lady was just, like, at *peace* after that. Really amazing."

I glanced back at Nils in my rearview. He was shaking his head.

"Do you have, like, specific questions you wanna ask the guy?"

"Specific questions?"

"Yeah, like, I mean, do you want to ask your mom something specific? Or maybe you want to ask about your future? I always want to know about my love life. My cousin took me to this guy once who does Tarot. Incredible. So crazy accurate. He totally predicted I was gonna date this guy—I can't tell you *who* because you guys sort of know him—but anyways, I did, I dated him. And he had predicted our problems and everything. So crazy."

I pushed down on the brake, then shifted the car into first. "I don't have any specific questions, I don't think. I just want to know if she exists still." I turned into Nora's driveway and pulled the car to a stop.

"Well, good luck, Holly. Let me know how it goes." Nora got out of the car. Nils stayed put. "You coming?" she asked. She was standing in her driveway now, one hand resting on her hip, her body bent over so she could see inside my backseat.

"I don't feel great," Nils said, stepping out of the car and onto Nora's pebble paved driveway. "I'll call you later."

"You're seriously not gonna come in?"

Nils opened the passenger side door, then slid in next to me. "I'll call you," he said again.

She nodded. But then she just stood there. I waved sheepishly, pushing down on the gas, watching her shrink smaller and smaller in my rearview the farther away we drove.

"Why'd you do that?" I asked.

"Do what?" said Nils, buckling his seat belt.

"Why'd you just leave her there like that? Didn't you guys have plans?"

"I guess." He picked at a microscopic zit on his chin. "We have plans every day, though. And she was annoying me."

"Annoying you how?"

"Holly, it's not that big a deal. I know what you're thinking, but it wasn't just the psychic thing. She's been bugging me all week." He rolled up his window. "Anyways, I'll see her tomorrow."

We drove and we drove and we drove without talking, then I slowed the car to a stop, slipped the stick shift into neutral and tugged on the emergency brake. We were home. "Do *I* annoy you?" I asked, laughing in an effort to undercut the desperation in my voice.

Nils unbuckled his seat belt and turned his whole body toward me. "Why would you ask me that?"

I shrugged, turning off the ignition. "Just suddenly feeling a little . . . I dunno. I need a boost, please."

"Holly. You don't ever annoy me. You could never annoy me."

I looked at him.

"Day after day and I never get sick of seeing your face," he said, grabbing me by my chin. Then he looked at me in this funny way that made my stomach go bananas. I don't know why. And he must have felt it too, because after that he snatched his hand away superquick and got out of the car.

Most of that weekend I kept to myself. I lay on the couch with Harry and watched *Mystery!* on PBS. I went to the farmers' market with Jeff and bought corn and heirloom tomatoes and homemade soap.

I hadn't spoken to Paul since Friday under the bleachers. So when it came time for World History/arts and crafts, Monday morning, I made it a point to be super friendly to Saskia. Just to spite him, I guess.

"How was your weekend?" I asked, looking down at our collage.

"Oh, good. I just . . . I went shopping with my mom and my brother on Saturday," she said, shaking a bottle of Elmer's glue down and around, slamming the narrow orange bottle tip against her desk. "Is this thing empty?" she asked, unscrewing its lid and peering inside. "It's empty," she concluded, tossing the bottle aside. "Sunday was fun, though." She was grinning now, absentmindedly running her fingertip over the pointy corner on our poster board. "I spent the day with Paul."

My stomach lurched.

"What about you?" she asked. She was wearing this tattered gray sweatshirt that was sort of frayed at the collar and I wondered whether it had been distressed by some trendy clothes manufacturer or by good old-fashioned time and abuse.

"Oh, I don't—it was quiet." I shrugged. "I just hung out with my dad and the dog."

Saskia flashed her teeth and handed me a photocopied cutout from our textbook. I coated the back with rubber cement and flattened it to the collage.

"What about your boyfriend?" she asked.

"Boyfriend?" I knew she couldn't have been asking about Paul. Still, I got goose bumps.

"Yeah, that guy Nils."

I exhaled, relieved. "Nils isn't my boyfriend."

"Really?"

"Nope."

Saskia pursed her lips and then I held our collage out at arm's length. We were halfway through our time line. "Now that right there . . ."

"A masterpiece," she deadpanned, grabbing the rubber cement off my desk.

This is the exact moment when I really started liking her,

watching her push her hair behind her ears, painting paper with rubber cement. She was nothing like I thought she'd be. She had a personality. "You're nothing like I thought," I said.

She looked at me crooked, raising an eyebrow. "Why? What'd you think I was like?"

"You know." I touched my hair. "The hair and the clothes. I just thought . . ."

"You thought what?" She screwed the cap back on the glue, her whole body going stiff.

"No! No, I mean, you're just so put together. I didn't think you'd be so nice, is all."

She relaxed. "Oh. Thanks. I think."

I can't explain why I suddenly loved her so much. It's not like we'd reached deep inside each other's souls or hearts or whatever. I still didn't know anything about her.

Saskia took out a piece of paper and scribbled something down. "Here."

"Hmm?"

"You should call me sometime."

"Call you?" I was confused. Why would I possibly call her?

The bell rang. She handed me the little slip of loose leaf. "My number. If you wanna hang out ever. Go to the beach or something." She stood up.

"Yeah, sure. Okay." I stood up too, stunned, watching as she pushed her desk against the wall before waving quickly and circling out into the corridor. I fingered the little slip of loose leaf between my thumb and pinkie finger, then slipped it into my back pocket before swinging my desk back into place.

Tap tap tap.

I sat up and stared groggily at Paul's face, which looked to me as if it were hanging in midair, floating around without a body.

I rubbed my eyes, then pressed a palm to my bedroom window. Paul kissed the glass.

"What're you doing here?" I asked. He shook his head and plugged his ears. *I can't hear you,* he mouthed. So I got out of bed and tiptoed down the hall, past sleeping Jeff, and Harry, who was up, wagging his tail. I cracked the door. "It's Monday," I whispered. He pushed past me, worming his way inside. "What're you doing here?" I asked. He put a finger to his lips and spun me around, pushing me back down the hall toward the bedroom, slipping my shirt over my head and then off with my pajama bottoms. "Are you still mad at me?" I asked, shoving my bedroom door shut with my elbow. He clamped a hand over my mouth and went back to undoing the buttons on his fly. "Mad?" he asked, kissing me again, sliding his free hand along the waistband of my orange cotton underwear, sending a warm jolt up my spine.

He pushed me backward onto the bed and hit my top lip. "Ow."

"Did that hurt?"

I touched my throbbing mouth, then shook my head. "Good."

Afterward, when we were through, we lay there like statues. I fell asleep for a bit, then woke up to some rustling around in my bed.

"Paul?" I heard my bedroom door click shut. I sat up. He was gone. So I got up on my knees and looked out the window. Paul was jogging down my driveway to his car, which he always parked on the street by our mailbox so no one would hear him coming and going.

I walked over to my stereo, slipped Neil Diamond into the CD player, and skipped to track nine. The first few bars of "Holly Holy" played softly as I fell backward onto my bed. Paul always spent the night. Always. He'd never left before without a quiet kiss or sweet good-bye.

I squeezed my eyes shut and tried not to cry. I tried and I tried until finally, I fell back to sleep, sometime around four thirty, about an hour and a half before I had to get up for school.

Chapter 16

The psychic called back.

It was after lunch on the way to Calc when my cell rang.

"Is this Holly?"

My hands shook, so stupid, I don't know why they were shaking, but I pressed the phone close to my ear and said, "Yeah, this is me."

"Frank Gellar." He sounded exactly like he had on his outgoing voice mail message. "You wanted to set up an appointment for a reading?"

I stopped moving and backed myself into the hallway wall. I had an immediate impulse to check my boobs for lumps but resisted the urge. "Yeah. Yes. I have, um . . . well, you're, like, a medium, right?" I pulled a notepad and pen from my backpack. "Like, I have someone that maybe I want to talk to—could you do that? Help me talk to that person?"

"I can certainly try." He coughed. "Did you want to book an hour session?"

"Is that what people normally do? How much is an hour?"

"One seventy-five."

I nearly choked on my spit. He didn't mean a dollar seventy-five, and I maybe had, like, tops, a hundred bucks stashed away in the sock drawer in my dresser. I knew I could've asked Jeff for the money but then Jeff would have asked me what I needed it for and I'd have to tell him *I'm trying to talk to Mom* and then what if he got mad like Nils did or worse, what if he cried?

"How much time could I get for a hundred bucks?" I asked.

"A half-hour session is ninety."

"Can we do a half hour then? This weekend?"

"I could take you on Saturday. At four?" I said four p.m. was fine, that it would work great and then he gave me the address to his house/office, which was pretty close by in the Palisades.

After that I felt absolutely great. I spent all of Calc thinking up questions I might want to ask come Saturday. Questions like, *Where are you? What does it look like where you are?* And *Please don't tell me how I'm going to die because I really don't want to know* (that last one isn't a question,

I guess). Then with five minutes left of class to spare, I drafted a note to Paul that said:

Hey you. I made an appointment for this Saturday at 4 pm with that psychic guy. Can you come, still? xoxo. Holly.

It was important to me that I seem warm and not angry after he'd left the night before without spending the night or saying good-bye. He'd promised to come with me to this thing and if he thought for a second I was mad or hurt he might retract his promise and I couldn't let that happen because I was scared to go alone.

Chapter 17

"I'm hungry."

"Holly, come on. Focus."

We were in Ballanoff's office drinking diet Snapple. He'd promised me extra credit in exchange for a thorough reading of *The Crucible*.

"Abigail Williams, right. Is she the witch?"

"Did you even read the play?"

I sunk down onto Ballanoff's desk so my upper arms and chin were flat against the tabletop. I picked up my copy of the play, then let it drop back down. "Sort of."

"Okay, so, themes, then. Go."

I blinked. "Witches?"

"Holly."

"What?"

Ballanoff clicked his pen against his top teeth, then rolled his eyes. "Fear. *Paranoia.* Power plays a significant role, here, don't you think?"

"Power, absolutely."

"So what does the John Proctor–Abigail Williams affair do for Abigail? How is she able to gain leverage, manipulate her town? What roles do power and sex and sexual repression play in the text?"

My stomach turned over. Words like "affair" and "sex" and "manipulate" now made me squeamish. "Look, I'm sorry, I didn't really read the whole thing, okay?" I sat up, abruptly, and shoved my copy of the play back into my bag. "Can we talk about something else instead?"

Ballanoff clucked his tongue, nodding unenthusiastically.

"Okay, good." I sat back, relaxing slightly. "Let's talk about . . ." I drummed my fingertips against his desktop. "How's about we discuss . . . you and my mom, again?" I winked.

"Again?"

"Again, yes," I said, leaning forward. "But this time, more details."

Ballanoff put one foot up on the edge of his desk and pushed backward in his chair. "Seriously, Holly, there's nothing to tell. It was *one* kiss."

"Yeah, but you knew her, right? What was she like back then? I mean, was she popular? Dorky? Did she have boyfriends? School spirit? What? Tell me something I don't know."

Ballanoff swallowed. "She was like . . . you know. She was like . . . *you*. I mean, she looked like you. Dark hair, pale skin. She was everyone's friend."

I snorted. "Oh yeah, just like me. Miss Congeniality."

"So true."

"Har har." I kicked the leg on his desk. "So?"

"So, what? So that's it."

"That's it? No more?" I darted my eyes down.

"She was just . . . she was really warm. And sincere. And people really responded to that, I think."

I looked back up. He was staring at me.

"Are you sure all you did was kiss?"

Ballanoff shifted around in his seat. "Holly, come on . . ."

I stared back, searching his face.

"There's no secret romance, here."

"Sure thing," I said, pushing my hair behind my ears, straightening up. "But, so . . . did you keep in touch? After graduation, I mean."

"Not really, I mean, I'd see her around on holiday breaks."

"With Jeff?"

"With Jeff, yeah." He nodded, downing the last of his diet iced tea.

"What's this about?"

Just home from my hike with Harry, and Jeff had the huge cardboard photo of my mother from her memorial service propped against the living room couch. I circled around it, touching its pointed edges.

"I don't know what to do with it. I was thinking maybe you and Nils would want it out in The Shack."

I looked at him with crazy eyes. "It's huge. It'll take up an entire wall in there. It'll be like a *shrine* to Mom." I kicked off my sneakers and padded across the kitchen floor in my socks. "No thank you."

He threw a chopped pepper into a hot wok. Smoke and oil flew up in front of his face. "Well, I don't know what to do with it. It's been in the bedroom for the past seven months and it's starting to make me agitated."

I walked over to the stove and picked up a slice of carrot. "Can I eat this?"

Jeff nodded.

"So why not just throw it out?"

He shook soy sauce over the vegetables. "I can't throw that out, Holly—it's huge. It's your mother."

"It's not her. It's a big piece of poster board." I took another carrot. "Besides, the picture is ugly. She was so beautiful and I love you, but your taste in photographs, not so good." I went on, my mouth full. "Please, don't ever do that to me. If I die, I want a nice photo that makes me look really great."

"Don't even joke, please. The thought of losing you . . ."

I grabbed Jeff's arm. "Oh, I'm kidding, come on." He

kissed my cheek and I took another carrot. "Why don't we stick it in the garage for now?"

Jeff nodded. I picked Mom up by her pointy corners and carried her down the front steps and around to the garage. I slid past Jeff's car and searched for a place to put her. On the other side of the washer there was a little bit of wall space. She'd fit perfectly. I propped her up against a big copper pipe and bent down to kiss her one-dimensional lips. "You'll have fun down here," I said to the photograph. "See you next time I do a load of whites."

Chapter 18

After school, I watched from the grassy hill above the parking lot as Paul approached his car. He was alone. I waved, loping forward.

"Holly," he said, only he didn't seem excited to see me.

"Did you get my note?" I asked, breathless from the downhill run.

He stuck his key into the car lock and opened the driver's side door.

"What note?"

"I left a note in your locker on Tuesday. About the psychic? It's tomorrow, my appointment."

"That's great." He got into his car, shut the door, and rolled down his window. "Thanks, but—I asked in the note If you could come with me. Remember you said you would come?"

"Oh, yeah, but I can't. Saskia's birthday is Sunday and I'm going with her family to Catalina for the weekend. It's gonna be awesome. We're camping."

"Oh."

He looked so happy about his dumb Catalina plans. Camping with Saskia and her sick brother and I just wanted to hurt him. I wanted to kick him and hurt him and make him cry, but instead I just stood there, eventually blurting, "But I don't want to go alone."

"So take Nils."

"Nils doesn't think it's a good idea."

"Well, Holly, I can't go. I mean I really feel for you, but you should have asked me before scheduling the appointment if you wanted me to come so bad."

"But I did ask you. I left you that note."

He started the car. "Well, I dunno, maybe I just didn't get it." But that was a lie. I was sure he got the note.

"Well, if I cancel and reschedule, will you come with me then? When would be better for you?"

"I really don't know. Just not tomorrow, okay? Next week's bad too."

I smiled but I didn't feel happy. I felt shitty and desperate but I said, "Okay," anyway.

So I cancelled the appointment and rescheduled with

Frank Gellar: Psychic Medium, for Saturday, the weekend after next, at three p.m. And I felt like a real pussy doing it but I wanted what I wanted. I wanted Paul there.

"I'm eating with you today," Saskia said, sticking a fork into her chickpea-iceberg lettuce salad and sitting down. My eyes darted to her usual table, where her friend Sarah something-or-other sat with a whole bunch of Saskia-types, eating and looking conspicuously happy. "Won't your friends miss you?" I asked, gesturing to her table.

"They can do without me for one day. Besides, you're much more interesting." She brought a forkful of salad to her mouth. I quickly looked around the room, scanning the place for Paul. He had class this block, I'd never seen him at Wednesday lunches, but still, I had to ask, "Where's your boyfriend?"

"Western Civ. He eats late lunch on Wednesday." She took another bite, talking and chewing and somehow still seeming adorable. "What about *your* boyfriend?" she teased, meaning Nils. I knew this now.

"He's *not* my boyfriend," I said. "But, him too. Late lunch. Wednesdays I usually eat alone and read."

She shoveled another bite of salad into her mouth. "Weekend plans?"

"What? No. Maybe I'll see a movie with my dad." I shrugged. "You?" I winced having to ask. I knew her weekend plans already.

She smiled sheepishly. "My birthday."

I feigned surprise and took a bite of sandwich. "No way!"

"Mm. We're going to Catalina."

"Oh, wow—"

"Camping."

"So great."

"We haven't been on a family trip in so long. And I get to bring Paul this time, so I'm psyched."

"Bet you are," I said, suddenly unable to meet her eye. I checked the clock on the wall. I looked at my bagged lunch, at her salad, down at my hands. I changed the subject. "Your family's big?" I asked.

She sunk back in her chair. "Not really. Me, Mom, step-dad. My brother."

"He's older? Your brother?"

"Technically, yes. He's nineteen. But I'm the older one, really. I'm the one who takes care of him, you know?" She polished off the last of her lunch. "Not the other way around."

I nodded, remembering Paul's words: Her brother was sick. I wondered what that meant, then said, "You really like lettuce, huh?"

She glanced down at her empty plate. "I like lettuce," she said, her shoulders shaking with laughter. "I really do."

Chapter 19

Nils and I were poking around Goodwill, drinking milkshakes out of tall paper cups.

"So, you'll be happy to know I'm gonna end it."

"End what?" I tugged a sequined dress off a rack packed with evening wear. "You think I could pull this off?"

"Where are you gonna wear that? To prom?"

"I'm not going to prom."

"Of course you're not."

I stuck the dress back on the rack. Nils ran his hand down the arm of a men's suit jacket that was hanging on the wall, displayed. "Did you hear what I said?"

"About the dress?"

"About me ending things. With Nora."

I stopped walking and turned around to face him. "You're gonna break up with her?"

"I'm bored."

"Does she know you're gonna break up with her?"

"She's got to see it coming. She can't possibly be having fun anymore. We have nothing to say to each other."

I turned back toward the rack of dresses and sipped my vanilla milkshake. "I feel bad for her."

"What do you mean, you feel bad for her? You hate her. You think she's dumb."

"Sure, she's dumb, but she has feelings. You know, clearly she's really into you. I just feel bad." *Poor Nora Bittenbender,* I thought, pulling at the skirt of a zebra-print dress, pondering Paul and me for a second or two. "So have you thought about how you're gonna do it?"

"Do it?"

"You know, break it off."

"Well, we're not even really together."

"So?"

"So I just figured I could slowly pull back—you know, that way no one really gets their feelings hurt."

I shook my head, incensed. "That's the shittiest thing I've ever heard. You can't do that. What, so, that girl goes around wondering whether she's still with you or not until she sees you screwing with some other poor, dumb girl—is that it? Just so you can spare yourself the awkwardness of having a fifteen-minute conversation where you say to her, 'I'm sorry you're sweet but this just isn't going to work out'??? What's wrong with you?" I spun on my heels and beelined for the display case at the front of the store.

Nils followed. "Hey! Hey, Crazy? You're acting insane." He grabbed me by my arm. "I'll break up with her, okay? Face-to-face. The whole 'pulling back' thing was just an idea."

I softened. I looked at him.

"What's with you? Are you okay? Why do you care so much about this all of a sudden?"

I shrugged. "I'm trying to be more compassionate, okay? I felt bad for her that day in the car when we just left her standing alone in her driveway."

Nils took a long sip from his drink. "You stand alone in your driveway all the time." He slipped an arm around my waist and drew me toward him. "Hey so, Paul Bennett?"

My insides went cold. "What about him?" I asked. I'd stopped laughing. *Does he know something? How could he possibly know something?* I squirmed free and hurried toward the front of the store.

Nils followed. "You know those glasses he wears? Those aviators?"

I was at the jewelry display now, fondling a string of faux pearls. "I don't know. I mean, I guess, yeah."

"He kept those things on all through Russell's lecture today. Who does that? Seriously. Who keeps their sunglasses on indoors? In *class*?"

"I dunno," I said quickly, nervously, trying on the fake pearls, then hanging them back on their hook. I pointed toward the display case, eager to change subjects. "See that necklace?"

"Which one?"

I touched the glass. "The one with green pendant."

"I see it, yeah."

"I think it would look great on me, don't you?"

We were both bent down now, looking at the necklace. Nils bumped his body against mine and I swayed to one side. "Sure I do. Green is your color."

I rolled out my hand. "Lend me ten bucks, moneybags? I spent the last of my cash on our milkshakes."

Nils pulled a twenty out of his pocket and placed it in my open palm. "You're the best," I said, cupping his cheek with one hand. "Excuse me," I called, flagging down the Goodwill store clerk with a wave of Nils's crisp twenty-dollar bill. "Can I see something in the display case?"

Nils lifted the lid off his cup, downing the remains of his shake. I watched him sideways, bracing myself for more Paul talk.

"What?" he asked, feeling my glare.

"Nothing," I countered, relieved. Then I turned back to the clerk, who was now hovering over the display case. I pointed at my necklace, exhaling.

Chapter 20

In eighth grade I found all Mom's old photo albums stashed away in the hall closet by the bathroom. I'd been bored that day and leafing through her secret collection of historical novels—a tall pile of paperback books devoted to Henry VIII and all his sexy wives, *Catherine of Aragon, Catherine Howard, Anne Boleyn*, buxom ladies in corsets she kept stacked in the back of the closet next to the shoe rack. I'd been skimming a book on Jane Seymour, jumping from chapter to chapter in search of sex scenes (I did this biweekly), when I noticed something new: next to her stack of paperback wives were three or four puffy maroon photo albums I'd never seen before. I picked one up, cracked the spine, and there, staring back at me, were photos of my mother with some dude I didn't recognize. He was hairy. He had a beard and wild hair and in every picture he was wearing the same pair of destroyed, bleached jeans.

"Who is this?" I asked. We were standing in the kitchen. Mom was eating grapes out of plastic carton in front of the fridge.

"Where'd you find that? My god, *me*, babe, that's me."

"No, I know that's you. I meant the guy. The hairy guy, who is he?"

"Oh." She popped another grape in her mouth. "That's Michael. My college *boyfriend*." She leaned into me, poking me in the ribs. I hated the word "boyfriend." "He's married now and lives in Calabasas." Mom stopped to think for a second or two before shoving the grapes back into the fridge and shutting the door.

"Can I borrow this?"

"Yeah, sure. Why?"

"I just want to look," I said, pressing my hand against the puffy cover, then racing down the hall to my bedroom.

Mom and Michael. So gorgeous. I loved their old clothes, tan skin, and slim bodies. I ran my hands across each page, fondling the edges of the yellowing clear plastic sheathing that lay over each collage of photos. I adored Michael: his hair, his jeans, the way he *gazed* at my mother in each photograph. They looked so happy together.

"So, okay. I don't get it."

This was later. We were out on the deck, in the sun,

drinking sparkling cider out of champagne flutes. Mine had a tiny umbrella hanging off the lip of my glass. I pushed it to one side, then took a sip of my drink. "Why'd you and Michael break up?"

Mom squirted a dollop of coconut-scented sunscreen into her palm and motioned for me to move closer. "What do you mean, *why*? I met your dad." Then, "Here, come'ere, let me do your back."

I scooched closer, positioning myself so she could smear cream across my back. "But, why? Didn't you love Michael? He really looked like he loved you."

"We were young, babe. We just . . . broke up. You know?"

"But you looked so happy with Michael."

"Aren't you glad Daddy and I got married?"

"Yes, of course, but I don't understand why things didn't work out with you and Michael."

She twisted her long hair into a knot and smiled at me with her mouth shut. "We both just . . . I don't know, babe, we both just loved other people more."

Chapter 21

"This is it, you know."

Nils and I were on our backs in The Shack.

"What is?" he asked.

We were lying side by side, fully clothed—jeans and sneakers—the two of us tucked in tight, cozy in our fleece-lined cocoons.

"*This.* No more nights in The Shack after this. It's over."

Every now and then, when Jeff had okayed it, we'd have sleepovers. Gross food, sleeping bags, bad music, Scrabble.

"We have till the end of summer, Hols."

I stuck my hand into a bag of Doritos and delicately bit the corner off a chip. "Yeah but, that's, like, two seconds away. And then we're done. You're gonna move to, like, Colonial Williamsburg or some nonsense and I'll still be here."

Nils laughed. "Rhode Island. *Maybe* New York."

"Whatever." I licked nacho cheese dust off my fingertips and flipped onto my side. "Are we still gonna talk? Once you're gone?"

"Holly, yes." Nils was on his back, staring at the ceiling.

"Why won't you look at me?"

He turned his head so we were face-to-face. "That better?"

"Much." I slipped another chip from the bag. We stared at each other for a minute.

"You still have that *thing* going on, Hols?" He turned back to the ceiling. "Whatever it was you couldn't talk about before?"

I sucked in some breath. "Sort of."

"How's that going?" he asked, cracking his knuckles.

I curled my knees to my chest and slipped off my sneakers. "Pretty shitty."

Nils faced me. "How so?"

I shook my head. I wanted to tell him. I wanted to tell him everything. I wanted to tell him how I wasn't a virgin anymore and how it wasn't just that I'd had sex *one time* but I'd had sex multiple times—hundreds, it seemed like. And how in the beginning it had hurt so bad I could have screamed but that Paul was so amazingly sweet he'd made up for any real pain I'd felt. And how now that time had passed and sex seemed suddenly easy, I'd somehow managed to make up for any physical pain with barrelfuls of emotional pain that seemed directly proportionate to the amount of pleasure I took in the actual act. I suspected I was being punished. Possibly by my mother. Most definitely by god.

"You haven't, like, brought whoever it is *here*, have you?"

"What? No. Never. We've already talked about this." I sat up and leaned forward, running a finger over Mom's CDs, all stacked nicely on the shelf Jeff had built. "What do you want to listen to?"

"Anything. You choose."

I pulled a Leonard Cohen CD off the shelf and slipped it into the stereo. I hit play.

Nils went on. "Do you really like this person?"

I thought about it. "I do."

"Would *I* like this person?"

I laughed. I considered Nils's total disdain for Paul. "Absolutely not."

"Is he nice to you?"

I dug my nails into Nils's shoulder and shook him back and forth. "Nils, stop. Come on. Stop asking me."

"I just don't understand why we can't talk about this."

I didn't say anything. I turned my back to him. After a minute or so I changed the track on the Leonard Cohen CD and then Nils said, "Is that it? We're done?"

I dug a ponytail holder out of my jeans pocket and twisted my hair into a knot. I changed the subject. "Have you given any more thought to Nora Bittenbender?" I asked.

He reached over and took my hand, pulling me close. "I'm not gonna do it until after her birthday party. She's so psyched about that thing. I'd wreck everything."

"What're you going dressed as?" I asked.

"Don't know yet. Maybe a vampire. Or a chicken."

"A chicken?" I backed myself into him, dragging the sleeping bag up to my chin. "You're so weird."

"You?"

"Me what?"

"What're you gonna go as?"

I thought about it. "A sexy nurse. Or a sexy ghost, maybe. So long as it involves a bikini. I just want to fit in, you know?" I tried looking really sincere.

Nils covered my face with a pillow.

Chapter 22

Paul and I were in his car at the beach after school. He'd stopped coming by at night now, so this was it, basically. Once a week. The deserted beach parking lot. His cramped, shitty old ruby red Beamer. We didn't even talk anymore. Just *off with your clothes, Holly, I have a paper due on Monday.*

"I have that thing tomorrow."

"What thing?" He was stuffing his T-shirt into the waistband of his jeans.

"The appointment. With the psychic." I wasn't looking at him. I knew what his response would be but felt compelled to tell him anyways.

"Oh yeah?"

I straightened my skirt. "Remember you said you'd come with me?"

"I said that?"

I looked out the widow and watched a seagull pick at an open bag of pretzels lying next to an overstuffed trash can. "You did."

Paul lit a cigarette. "Well, I can't go. I have a family thing."

"What sort of family thing?"

"Company family picnic thing at my mom's work. I have to go."

"Okay," I said. I continued to watch the seagull.

Paul poked me in the side. "That's it? No ball busting? Holly, so unlike you . . ."

I leaned my forehead against the window. "Well, you know. I figured as much."

"You still gonna go?" he asked, lighting a cigarette and starting the car.

"I am," I said, then I thought about Nora Bittenbender. I thought about Nils. I turned and looked at Paul. "What happened to you?" I asked.

"What do you mean?" He turned out of the beach parking lot and onto the PCH.

"You used to be so nice."

"You don't think I'm nice anymore?" He slipped a hand around my neck, the cigarette pinched between his lips.

"I really don't," I said, shoving his hand away.

"You're too sensitive, Holly. Nothing happened to me. I've always been this way."

I tugged on my seat belt. "Remember when you drove me into L.A.?"

"Of course I do. It wasn't that long ago."

"Remember when you promised me you'd come see this psychic guy with me?"

"Holly, come on." He clamped his thumb and pointer finger around the filter on his cigarette and flicked a millimeter of ash off the tip.

"What?"

"I'm sorry I broke my promise, okay? Doesn't change anything. I still can't go."

"What if I were someone else?"

"Like who?"

"Like someone you liked more."

"Holly, come on, stop it. Why do you torture yourself? The relationship I have with you is completely different from the one I have with her."

"No kidding."

"Two totally separate things."

"Apples and oranges," I cracked, feeling nauseated.

"Exactly." He ruffled my hair. I thought about Saskia. Her great face and cheery disposition. "She could do a lot better than you," I said.

He reached across the seat and slid a finger under my chin. "Oh yeah? What about you, Holly?"

I shrugged. "I'm guessing this is about what I deserve."

Paul flicked his cigarette out the open window. I propped one leg up on the dash.

After I got dropped off, I did something I know I shouldn't have done. I plopped down on my living room floor, dumped the entire contents of my book bag out onto Mom's pretty red woven rug, and there, amidst the heap of plastic folders, spiral notebooks, loose Tic Tacs and tampons, was the crumpled little piece of loose-leaf Saskia had written her phone number on, just weeks before. I smoothed out its creases, fished my cell out of my pocket, and dialed. It rang. And it rang. And then, just as I was prepping myself to leave a message on her voice mail, she picked up. "Hello?"

"It's Holly."

"Holly!" Such surprise. "Hi."

I knew she'd be alone. I knew that even if Paul had left me and gone directly to her, I had, at minimum, a twenty-minute window before he'd reach her doorstep.

"I'm sorry to call."

"Holly, why? I'm glad. That's why I gave you my number. So you'd use it. What's up?"

I didn't know how to say what I wanted to say, so at first, I didn't say anything. Then that made things awkward, so finally I just blurted, "I have this thing I have to do tomorrow and I can't go alone."

"What is it?"

"You're gonna think I'm crazy."

"I won't. Tell me," she said. Quickly followed by, "Wait, hold on a sec, I'm going outside." I heard a screen door squeak and then slam. "Okay. I'm ready. Go ahead."

So I told her about the psychic. How I'd been looking for signs from my mother. How I'd made this appointment and how I was scared to go alone and that it was scheduled for tomorrow at three and would she be willing to come along?

"Of course I would. I'd love to go," she said.

My whole body relaxed. I felt fantastic. I had a friend.

I spent the morning preparing myself. I woke up and went out to The Shack and imagined Mom on the cloud and I talked to her. I said, *I'm going to see this guy today and he's going to make it so you and I can have an actual conversation and if it's really you coming through, say something about Harry. I'll know it's you for real if you just say something cute about Harry.* Then I went inside and cooked breakfast for Jeff. I ate strips of bacon standing up while rehearsing in my head the things I wanted Frank Gellar to ask my mom. Mainly just: *Is your fate my fate?* And: *Why won't you send me a sign?* Then I twiddled my thumbs, watched an episode of *The Twilight Zone*, and ate a small bag of cherry tomatoes. Then, at two fifteen, I left to pick up Saskia.

I hadn't been to her house in about six years. But it looked exactly the same from the outside. Pink adobe. Big. Old. I got out of the car and followed a trail of wide, flat rocks to her doorstep and rang the bell.

Fifteen seconds later, the door swung open. There she was, blindingly blond. She smiled, hugged me hello, and followed me back out to my car.

"I forgot to mention . . . can you please not tell anyone about this?"

She was buckling her seat belt. "Don't worry, I won't." She drew a cross over her heart with her polished pointer finger.

"Not even your brother, or like, Paul, for example. . . ." *Especially not Paul, please god NO, not Paul,* I thought.

"I'm very trustworthy," she insisted.

Unlike me.

I started the car.

Frank Gellar's place wasn't all that impressive, but his neighborhood was a suburban dream. Sidewalks and tidy gardens with clay gnomes and multicolored pinwheels. I pulled the car to a stop and rechecked the street number.

"Is that it?" Saskia asked, pointing out the window at the small, brown house.

"That's the one," I said. We looked at each other.

"What time is it?"

I checked the digital clock on my dash. "Two fifty." I paused. "Maybe we could just sit here for a bit. We still have time."

"Whatever you want to do."

I turned on the radio and searched for a good song but couldn't find anything I liked. Saskia talked a little bit about her stepdad but I was distracted and couldn't hear what she was saying. I watched while she spoke, her lips sliding over her smooth white teeth. Then I pulled two pieces of cinnamon gum out of the glove compartment.

"You ready? It's almost three."

"I feel sick," I said. I did. Suddenly. My stomach was looping around itself like an unbalanced washing machine.

"You want something? A mint?" She opened her purse and started fishing around inside.

I grabbed her hand. "What if he tells me something I don't want to hear?"

"Like what?"

"I don't want to know how I'm going to die."

"He won't tell you that."

"But what if he does?" I looked at her. "Or what if he can't make contact at all? What if she's just, like, not there . . . ? Or anywhere?" I swallowed, continuing. "Let's say he *does* make contact, great, *awesome*, only she's not at peace. What if"—I tightened my grip on Saskia's hand—"what if I'm not living up to her expectations. She might be disappointed in me."

Saskia didn't say anything for a minute and then she put her face close to my face. "No way. Your mom is proud. Look at you, Holly." She fixed her eyes on me.

I sucked in a whole bunch of air. "I don't want to go in."

"What? Why?"

"I just don't. I can't."

Saskia looked at me for a bit. "You sure?"

"Yes."

She paused. "You hungry?"

"Not really."

"Eating always helps when I feel nauseous. Burritos are especially soothing."

I turned the ignition and rolled down my window. "Burritos? Really?"

"Bean and cheese. Trust me." She picked her phone out of her purse. "You want me to call this guy and cancel?"

"Call him," I said, passing her his card then pulling a quick U-turn.

We sped back toward Sunset, stopping at Pepe's on our way to the beach. Saskia bought me a bean and cheese burrito and a potato taco for herself.

I ate my burrito in the car.

The beach with Saskia was different from the beach with Paul. It felt more like the beach had felt with my mom when I was a kid. We lay on our backs in the sand. Clothes on, shoes off. We made sand angels.

"Do you regret leaving?" she asked me, shielding her eyes from the sun with one hand.

I thought about it. "I feel relieved."

"Relieved, really?" She turned onto her side.

I shrugged, picking up a handful of sand.

Saskia didn't say anything for a while, then said, finally, "I'm glad you asked me, anyway."

I looked at her.

"I mean I'm glad you called."

I grinned. I dug some sand out from beneath my thumbnail.

"My brother," she said, looking down. "He has this . . . kind of *issue* with depression." She picked at her cuticles.

"Oh."

"And when you told me about the psychic I kind of wondered how I'd feel knowing my own destiny. Or knowing Sean's destiny. Like if I knew he'd be fine one day? Maybe then I could relax and stop worrying. Seems so nice, not having to worry." She lay back down. "It's like my *dream*," she said, which made me feel really sad.

"Has he always been like that? Depressed?"

She nodded. "He's always been medicated. But lately he's just been extra bad. He hides stuff. . . ." She took a breath. "It all sounds so dramatic, I know."

I watched her for a while as she drilled her finger into a little hole in the sand. Drilling and *drilling* and then she pulled her finger back and flicked a few stray grains of sand out from under her pinkie nail. She looked so ladylike doing it too. And she must have felt me watching her because suddenly she was peering up, asking, "What?! What's wrong?" So I said, "Nothing," and she just made a face at me, then went back to picking her cuticles.

I thought about Paul. Then about Paul and Saskia together. He wasn't with her because she'd *break* if they broke up. It wasn't because her brother was crazy or because she couldn't survive on her own. Being with her had nothing to do with some misguided sense of moral obligation. He was with her because he loved her. Of course, and who wouldn't? *I* loved her. It was sudden and unexpected but it was true. *I would trade him for her*, I thought. *In an instant.*

I slid my hand over the stiff material of my jeans. I felt happy. Grateful. I'd lose a boy but I'd gain a friend. The choice was clear.

Paul had to go.

Chapter 23

At first, I didn't really do anything different. I just stopped paying attention to him. Every time I thought about him I'd think about *her* instead. What I'd be losing if I continued to see him—a real friend. One that I didn't share a tool shed with. Or feed Snausages to after school.

So when Paul didn't look at me when we passed each other in the hall on Monday, I tried not to care. And when Tuesday came and went without a visit to my bed, I danced around my bedroom to Mom's albums instead.

On Wednesday, though, Wednesday he was out by my car, waiting for me in the school parking lot after gym. "Hi," he said, leaning in for a kiss.

"Aren't you scared someone might see?" I quipped.

"No one's around, come on." He dragged me forward by the waistband on my shorts.

"Don't." I squirmed, pulling at his fingers.

"You look great, though . . . all sweaty." He grinned and ruffled my hair. "Let's go to the beach. Come on, I'll drive."

I took a step back. "I can't go to the beach with you."

"Why not?" He lit a cigarette, inhaled extra deep, and slipped the lighter back into his shirt pocket.

"I just don't feel good about it anymore. I want to stop."

"Stop what?"

I darted my eyes down. I thought if I looked at him for too long I might not be able to say what I had to say. "Seeing each other. We can't see each other anymore."

Paul wasn't saying anything, so I glanced up.

He was fidgeting with the lid on his Zippo. "Why not?"

"A lot of reasons."

"Like?"

"Like . . . it's not really good for me, I don't think."

"What about me?"

"What *about* you?"

"Don't I get a say?"

"You have a girlfriend. You don't need me."

He wrapped one arm around my waist and pulled me into him. "Maybe I want you."

"I see you *once* a week," I scoffed. "You don't even talk to me anymore."

"Is this about the psychic?"

We were still standing close, his arm around my hips. "I just think it's wrong."

"Wrong."

"Yes. *Girlfriend*," I said again, slow and loud, hoping he'd hear me this time.

He leaned forward to kiss me. And I'm not sure why, but I let him. Then I stepped backward, pulled my keys out of my book bag, and said, "I have to go."

"So that's it?"

I got into my car and slammed the door shut. Then I rolled down my window and looked at him.

He said, "You think this is over, but it's not."

You're wrong, I thought. Then I turned the ignition and put the car into first. "See you around," I said, laying into the gas pedal.

Chapter 24

Saskia and I were in the hills by my house, winding up a narrow, dusty path covered with dry brush and pricker bushes. It was dark out.

"What time is it?"

"I dunno. Not late. Eight?" I guessed.

Saskia skipped around me and ran up ahead toward a clearing at the top of the hill. "You wanna sit for a bit?" she asked, breathless from the climb.

"Okay." I nodded, hiking up the extra ten yards or so. She was kneeling in a puddle of dusty dirt. I dropped down next to her. For a minute or two we just sat side by side, breathing dry air.

"We're lucky, huh?"

"Why's that?" I asked, pulling on a dead root, ripping

it out of the ground and snapping it in two.

"All this?" she pointed at our view: mountains, ocean, dry grassy hills and valleys. "We lived in New York when I was a kid. Until I was, like, six or so? Suburbia. Nothing like this. I mean, there were beaches, but they were different. And it was flat."

I nodded. I'd never been to New York. I'd only ever lived here and couldn't imagine life outside Southern California. I broke my dead root into fours.

"Look, planes," said Saskia, pointing at the tiny blinking lights floating over the ocean. There were four or five at least, small specs of light that barely looked as if they were moving. "They look like fireflies," she said, sinking further down to the ground.

"I've never seen a firefly," I said.

"Yeah, we don't have those here, do we?"

"Nope."

"Well, they look like that," said Saskia, pointing at the glowing dots of light speckled over the sea. "Exactly. They're small and they blink like planes do. That's the one thing I miss. Bugs"—she laughed—"that glow."

"They sound unreal. Like magic critters."

"They are," she said, turning to face me. "That's exactly what they are," she murmured, pulling on a lock of long, sandy hair.

Chapter 25

When I was really small, before we lived in the house we have now, Jeff, Mom, and I lived in one of those two-story townhouse complexes by the beach. I don't remember much about that place other than the ocean out back, our spiral staircase, and this really red, rectangular table where we ate all our meals, but lately, I'd been thinking a lot about that apartment.

"You okay?"

Jeff and I were in the kitchen eating brown rice and beans. I took a sip of water. "Fine," I said. "Just thinking."

"About what?"

I'd been picturing dinners at that old apartment. Me, Mom, Jeff. Mounds of Italian takeout. I had the perfect memory fixed in my head: the three of us slurping spaghetti around our chintzy table. "Nothing interesting," I said. "School stuff. Do we have any soy sauce?"

"Fridge," Jeff said, taking a bite of rice.

I got up and shuffled forward, drifting back to my memory—spaghetti, old apartment—I swapped out my image of Jeff and replaced him with visions of Ballanoff—rewriting my memory so that the new version went something like: me, Mom, and Ballanoff, together, eating sizzling Szechuan chicken with chopsticks. "You want chili sauce?" I asked, my hand hovering over the huge orange bottle on the door of the fridge.

"Sure, yeah."

I grabbed both bottles and kicked the door shut with my sneaker sole. "Maybe we can get Chinese sometime this week."

"You want Chinese? I thought you didn't like Chinese."

"No, I do." I pictured Ballanoff lifting a white, doughy dumpling to his lips. "I like Szechuan chicken. Dumplings, too." I dropped back down in my chair, then slid the chili sauce across the table toward Jeff.

"Then, okay, yeah, sounds great, Hols."

I nodded, satisfied, lifting my cup to my lips.

Chapter 26

Tap tap tap.

I'd been asleep. I opened one eye and stared up at my window. *Tap tap tap.* Paul was wearing this ratty, old red T-shirt I'd loved. Still did. It was thin and had holes at the armpits.

"Holly," he mouthed. My window was shut.

"Go away," I said back. He'd been calling nonstop lately. Every day, sometimes twice a day. I hadn't been answering his calls.

He shook his head. I turned over so I was facing away from the window. *Tap tap tap. Tap tap tap.* I turned back around. "Holly," he said again. I sat up, slipped on my slippers, and ran down the hall to the front door. He was waiting when I got there. I cracked the door a smidge a slid outside.

"You have to leave," I whispered, folding my arms over my chest and leaning my back against the side of the house.

"I was a total asshole," he started. "Please, let me come in. I won't touch you. I just want to talk."

I stiffened.

"Come on, Holly. I'm like your fucking dog. Please"—he clamped his hands together as if he were praying—"let me come in."

"Just say whatever you have to say. And keep your voice down, Jeff's asleep."

"Let's go to the toolshed."

"No."

"Isn't that where you and your little boyfriend play house?"

I twisted toward the door. I was going back inside.

"Holly Holly Holly . . ." He pulled me back by my elbow. "I'm sorry, I'm just jealous, okay? I'm sorry."

He fished around in his pocket and pulled out a lighter and a pack of cigarettes. "I miss you," he said, lighting up.

I pulled my shorts down so they sat square on my hips and watched Paul puff out a big poof of smoke.

"And I'm sorry. And I want things to go back to the way they were."

I looked at the ground and kicked a pile of dirt.

"I'm gonna break up with her."

A bolt of fear shot up my spine. "You can't do that. Why would you do that?"

"For *you*."

"But I don't want you to." I looked down by Paul's feet and saw a rotten lemon. I rolled my foot over the moldy part and smashed it into the ground.

"Holly." His voice was pleading. I felt sick to my stomach. I wanted to take him inside and take off his clothes and sleep next to him all night long. But all his promises and declarations of everlasting adoration couldn't change the fact that he only wanted me because I wouldn't let him have me. "You have to go," I said.

He shook his head, took a long drag off his cigarette, and exhaled in my direction.

I opened my front door and went back inside. Then I watched from the kitchen window as he jogged back down the hill toward his car.

Chapter 27

Saskia's room was plastered with photos of her and her friend Sarah whose last name I could never remember. The twin bed she'd had as a kid had been replaced by a queen-size mattress and box spring with no bed frame or headboard. On her nightstand sat a stack of crappy fashion mags and next to that a picture of her and Paul together in the canyon somewhere.

"You guys are pretty close, huh?" I pointed at a collage hanging over her dressing bureau. "You and your friend Sarah, I mean."

"I guess, yeah."

I turned and walked toward her bed. "Did you know I was here once before?"

"You were?"

"In sixth grade, for your birthday party."

"I don't remember you being here. So weird."

I sat down on her bed. "Where's your brother?"

"Work, maybe?" She walked to the mirror, grabbed an elastic off the vanity, and pulled her hair back into a smooth ponytail. "You hungry?" she asked, whipping her whole body around to face me.

I nodded.

"Come here." Saskia took my hand and led me downstairs to the kitchen. She pulled a tub of guacamole out of the fridge and a bag of potato chips from the cupboard. We plopped down on the couch in the living room and ate the entire bowl, barely stopping to breathe between bites.

Afterward I lay on the floor, my hands resting on my stomach. Saskia was on the couch, still.

"Have you finished all your school applications?"

"Basically, yeah." She sniffed. "Have you?"

"Pretty much." I was applying to four schools, all in California, which wasn't the original plan, but Mom died and that put an end to any big dreams of leaving for snowy New York or whatever. So, three of my schools were in L.A. or nearby. One was up north, in Santa Cruz. "Doesn't matter much, anyway, I won't be going all that far."

"You're staying here?"

"Looks that way."

Saskia eyed me curiously.

"I feel guilty leaving Jeff."

"Oh."

I rolled over onto my front. "You know Ballanoff used to date my mom in high school?"

"No way, theater guy?"

"Yeah, theater guy."

"Gross, Holly."

I laughed. We lay there for a bit and didn't talk. My stomach gurgled.

"Holly?"

"Yeah?"

"Can I ask you something personal?"

"Yeah, sure." The cat came by and licked my face. I ran a hand down her smooth coat.

"Are you a virgin?"

I froze. My hand locked around the cat's neck. I shook my head—a slow *no*. "Why, what about you?" I asked, as a courtesy, a gesture, because I already knew the answer to that question.

"No," she whispered, biting at a hangnail.

No. No?

She went on. "Seriously though, sometimes I wish I *were*, still. We were so young when we started . . . *god*, and then once you start, you can't ever go back to just kissing or holding hands . . . sucks, right?" Saskia stretched her arms out, then flipped onto her side and looked at me. "I miss just . . . making out."

They had been having sex this whole time? My chest tightened. Maybe she meant someone other than Paul. "Who's 'we'?" I asked.

She flashed me a peculiar look. "Duh, *hello*, I'm not *that* big a slut." She chucked a pillow from the couch in my direction. "Paul." It missed me by a foot, landing by my feet. "Why, what about you?" She asked. "Who'd you do it with?"

"No one you know," I stammered quickly, a guilty wave slamming my gut. I sat up. "I feel sick," I said.

"You need the bathroom?" she asked, rushing over to help me up off the ground.

"It's okay," I gently swatted her hand away, stood up, and waddled off toward the toilet. "Be back."

I flipped on the fan, sat down on the edge of the tub, and cried. I hadn't cried in months. Not since Mom, and even then, I probably hadn't managed to squeeze out any more than a tear or two at her memorial. These, though, were big, soundless, sloppy tears. Unstoppable. Tear after tear, shooting down onto Saskia's bathmat like rain.

Knock knock knock. "You okay in there?"

I sucked in my breath, then blurted, "I'm good. Be out in a minute." Then I turned on the sink and splashed some water on my face, the way hysterical women in movies sometimes do. I fixed my hair and blew my nose and tried smiling at my reflection to see if I could pull off looking regular, but my eyes looked like puffy marshmallows.

I slinked back out the bathroom door with my head down.

"Are you okay? Have you been crying?"

I tried looking chipper. "No I just, I tried to make myself puke, which like, always makes my eyes tear. Anyways, it didn't work. I couldn't throw up."

"You want some ginger ale?"

"I should go home," I said.

"You sure?"

"Yeah. I'll just go home and sleep it off. This happens sometimes," I lied.

Chapter 28

I went dressed like a cat.

There was a piñata, a cooler full of orange soda and Coke, and four small bottles of bourbon being passed around for kicks. Nils and I were perched up high on the wooden railing of the deck, looking down on—I'm gonna guess—fifty kids, maybe sixty. Most of our class was there.

"So when's the big breakup scene gonna happen?"

Nils was wearing a chicken costume. Meaning he wore a fake beak and had a feather tucked into the chest pocket of his button-down. "Tomorrow," he said, sounding cheerless. "After this whole mess is over."

I looked out at the crowd. Saskia and her group, decked out in Girl Scout garb, were drinking in a circle on the ground by the azaleas. Paul was there too. Wearing a fedora and suit.

"Have you thought about what you're gonna say?"

Nils shrugged. "'You're a great girl. I can't handle a relationship right now. I'm not ready to commit.' Pretty standard stuff." He looked at me. "How's *your* situation?"

"Good, actually. Over."

"Wow. Really."

"Yup." I sat up straight. "I feel pretty great about it."

Nils looked at me as if he was going to say something, but then didn't.

"What're we doing here, anyways?" I asked, turning back toward the party. Watching Paul watch me from his spot on the grass.

"Who knows," said Nils. Then, "Hey, look. There's Paul Bennett!" He feigned enthusiasm. "Dude's wearing a fedora. What a loser."

Sudden nausea. I looked off in another direction. Nora was darting around the lawn in a Laker Girl cheerleading uniform. Midriff and thighs, very bare! I swung my legs over the railing and hopped down onto the grass. "Shall we mingle?" I asked. "Find some booze for our drinks?" I tapped my Coke can.

Nils jumped off the railing and dropped down next to me. He grabbed my hand and held it for a second. Longer than a second. Weird, because we hadn't ever really held hands before and it wasn't like Nils was drunk or anything. He didn't let go until Nora came by fifteen seconds or so later. She threw the full weight of her body against Nils's body, knocking our hands apart.

"Baby," she cooed, grabbing him by the back of his head and pulling him into a sloppy kiss.

"Having fun?" Nils asked, righting himself. Pushing his beak back onto his nose.

"A blast." She turned toward me. "Holly!!! I'm so glad you're here!" She lurched forward then, arms outstretched. We embraced. "You want whiskey?" She pulled a skinny bottle of Jack out from under her halter.

"Sure thing."

Nils and I held out our Coke cans. Nora poured.

I was drunk. Not really *drunk* drunk, just tipsy, and Nils was off with Nora somewhere, so I was alone, standing by the snack table eating a handful of chips when Saskia stumbled over holding a lily. "Are you drinking?" she asked, leaning forward.

I held the soda can to my lips and nodded. "What's that?" I pointed to the flower.

"I picked it."

"I can see that. I'm sure Nora's parents will be pleased once they see someone's picked all their lilies."

Saskia stuck the flower behind her ear. "Only one." She flung an arm around my shoulder and pulled me close. "Is this a fun party?"

"Not really," I said, quickly scanning the place for Paul. No sign of him. Not that it mattered now, whether he saw us together or not.

"I didn't think so." She kept her arm draped around my shoulder as we swayed from side to side. "I'm so glad to know you, Holly Hirsh." She pulled me closer and I let her. I loved how she loved me.

After that I found Nils, then lost him again, then waited in line for the bathroom forever, then got fed up and wandered back outside. I surveyed the crowd. All drunk. It was late. I wandered away from the party, through a heavily wooded area and found a nice spot behind an overgrown patch of jasmine. I pushed my leggings and underwear down around my ankles and squatted.

"Is that you?" came a disembodied voice.

I screamed, jumped up, and accidentally peed all over my legs.

"Holly, I know it's you, I'm coming back there." It was Paul.

I quickly hiked up my underwear and leggings. Paul appeared from behind a bush. "Hi."

"What're you doing back here?"

"Detective work . . ."

"Is that what you are?"

"A detective, yes. Like my hat?"

"I guess." I stepped backward into a tangle of weeds.

"Got a minute?"

"Not really."

"That blond girl back there? The one dressed like a Girl Scout . . . you know her?"

I froze momentarily, said, "Don't be a loser," then walked toward him. "Come on, let's go back to the party."

"What, so you're, like, best friends all of a sudden?"

"You're drunk, Detective Bennett. We can talk later, okay?" I tried pushing past him. He grabbed my arm.

"I miss you."

I shook my arm loose. "You don't miss me. You had me and didn't want me." I walked ahead. "Besides, you lied. You lied about sleeping with Saskia."

"I didn't lie."

"You did, you lied."

"Holly, come on, *wait*." He grabbed my arm again and spun me around.

"I have to go find a bathroom."

"I want to talk to you."

"Not now."

"Holly."

"What?!" I whipped around, waiting. Tapping my foot against a pile of dry, crunchy leaves.

"I think I should tell her."

My chest tightened. "Tell her what?"

"About you and me."

"There is no you and me."

"Holly."

"You can't."

"No, I can. I'm going to. This is good, see? It'll be out there then and no one has to feel guilty or bad anymore. What's that saying? About truth and freedom?" He started back toward the party. I grabbed him by the shirt and tried pulling him backward, but he just kept moving forward. So I flung myself on him, wrapping my arms around his neck from behind. He stopped. "Holly, what the hell?" He turned to face me. We were nose to nose.

"Please, you can't. It'll crush her. I've never had a friend like her before. She'll hate me." He took me by the chin. I pushed his hand away and took a breath. "Don't tell her. Please."

"I have to."

"No, you don't. Please, Paul? Whatever you want. I'll do it."

"Whatever I want?"

I nodded.

He took a step forward and pushed my shirt collar to the side so that it hung off one shoulder. Then he snapped my bra strap and laughed. My eyes welled up and went blurry. "Come on, Paul, *please*."

"Seriously, Holly, pull yourself together." He took my hand as if he were being nice. "You mull it over, okay? Things either go back to how they were or I tell Saskia about you and me. I'm giving you a week." He kissed me quick on the mouth and walked off.

I wiped my face, picked a twig off my sweater, and made my way back to the party. Nils was sitting Indian style on a cooler eating candy out of the broken piñata. He was talking to that Sarah girl.

"Hey." I tugged on the sleeve of his shirt.

He looked up, "Where've you been?"

"Can we go, please? It's late."

Nils stood up.

We walked home. It was a short walk, half a mile, maybe. I made Nils hold my hand all the way to my front door.

"'Night, Hols." He turned away from me, heading back across the yard to his house.

"Nils?"

He twisted back around.

I was sobbing. Suddenly. That same sort of breathless, silent crying I'd been doing days before in Saskia's bathroom. I felt my throat constrict and waved my hands in front of my face. Nils ran over.

"I can't breathe," I shrieked, fanning my hands, treading the ground beneath me. Nils took me by the waist and walked me over to The Shack. We went inside, he sat me down on the futon, and plugged the Christmas lights into the wall socket. "Should I go get Jeff?"

I shook my head and pulled him down next to me. "I did a really bad thing. I did something really bad to someone I really care about."

"Who?"

"Just promise you won't hate me. Ever. No matter what happens. Please?"

"I could never hate you. You're my best friend."

I nodded as if to say *thank you I love you you're my best friend too* but I couldn't get the words out.

Nils pulled me forward and I collapsed into his chest. I cried and I cried and with each silent sob his shirt grew more and more transparent with my snot and salty tears.

"Holly, what's going on? I won't tell anyone, please."

I sat up and took a deep breath and held it for as long as I could before exhaling. "I'm okay," I said.

"You're okay?"

I nodded. I could breathe. "I'm sorry about this. I'm sorry, you must think I'm nuts."

Nils looked at me funny.

"Don't look at me like that," I said, pursing my lips. "I know what this seems like."

"What's that?"

"Like I'm falling apart. I'm not, though. I'm okay."

Nils shook my shoulder. "You say so."

I stood up. "I'm good to go back to the house now."

"You sure?"

I nodded. "Thanks for this. For your shirt." I gestured to his tear-soaked T-shirt.

"You need me, Hols . . ." He took his cell out of his pocket and waved it around like a flag.

"S'okay. I should be able to get through the night."

I leaned forward and kissed his cheek. "You're the best," I said, pushing backward onto the squeaky toolshed door. "Really," I said. "No one better."

Chapter 29

Monday back at school was a total disaster. I was so paranoid I could barely see straight. Spotting Paul in the hall I almost had a seizure. All he did was pass by with a wink and a smile and I was certain the whole school knew everything.

World History wasn't much better. I spent the first ten minutes of class trying to read Saskia for signs that she knew something. My hands shook like leaves under my desk. My T-shirt was spotted with tiny patches of sweat. I didn't calm down or dry off until finally Saskia turned to me and said, "Are you okay? You look sick."

Sweet relief. She'd spoken actual words to me. They were nice words, full of caring and friendship. They sounded nothing like *you lying, boyfriend-stealing bitch!*—which were the words I'd prepped myself to hear that morning when I'd gotten dressed and ready for slaughter. I mean, school.

By lunchtime I'd calmed down slightly. Nils and I ate alone. Same old routine. Avocado and soy cheese sandwiches.

"Feeling better?" he asked, taking a bite of my sandwich.

"I wouldn't say better. I'd say *different*." My eyes darted over to Saskia and Paul's table. Everything seemed the same. Salad, french fries, excessive PDA.

"Have you done the deed yet?" I asked Nils, nibbling at a piece of crust that had fallen from my sandwich.

"I couldn't. Saturday she was way too hung over and Sunday I was helping my dad with the car." He brought his thumb to his mouth and chewed at a hangnail. "We have an open period together next block. I was thinking I'd talk to her then."

"At school?"

"Why, you think that's bad?"

"Maybe wait till *after* school?"

Nils nodded. "Right, after school . . . you're probably right."

I met with Ballanoff before Drama. We sat side by side on the edge of the stage. I kicked my legs back and forth.

"You ready for your scene?"

"I guess."

"Did you finish the reading?"

"I've been a little preoccupied."

"I Iolly, come *on*—"

"I'm sorry, *god*, I've got a lot on my mind."

"Oh yeah? Like what?"

I watched the auditorium doors. "Oh, you know."

He cocked his head. "I should flunk you."

"You wouldn't dare."

"You're probably right."

I gripped the edge of the stage with both hands. "Have you ever done something really bad?"

He gave me a small shrug. "Sure, I have."

"No, like, *really* bad. Have you ever, like, betrayed a friend?" I looked at him.

"I have, yeah."

"And you survived it?"

"I guess. I'm here, right?"

I considered him. "Do you ever get over the guilt?"

"Well, I guess it depends."

"On what?"

"Lots of things. To start . . . I mean, I suppose it depends on the deed done. "

I tried to picture Ballanoff doing something really bad. I pictured him in a black beret stealing jewels. And then again in a black beret stealing art. I laughed.

"What's so funny?"

"Nothing. I just can't imagine you doing anything bad." I paused. "Come on, tell me. What'd you do?"

He leaned forward. He whispered, "None of your business."

I nodded, looked down, and laughed. A few kids started trickling into the auditorium for class. "I'll finish the reading this week," I said, sliding off the edge of the stage and onto the carpeted floor.

Chapter 30

Blame it all on Paul's threats and my growing guilty conscience, but the week following Nora's party was record breaking for me in terms of alcohol consumption. Beer, whiskey, Kahlúa, more beer. *Puke*, Kahlúa. But you know the saying: *Desperate times . . .*

I was home Wednesday night, cleaning up dishes after dinner with Jeff, when Nils came by.

"Hi, hi." Jeff and I both got separate hellos. Nils bounced across the room and hopped up onto the countertop right next to kitchen sink. I passed him a wet dish and a towel. "Dry, please."

He winked and leaned toward me. "Can he hear us over here?"

"I can hear you over there," Jeff said, not moving from his station at the computer.

I snickered.

"I'm heartbroken," Nils announced loudly. "I broke up with Nora just now."

"Oh please," I passed him another dish. "You're the heart-*breaker*. You don't get to be broken."

Nils went on. "I wanna camp out tonight in The Shack. With Holly. Jeff, please?"

"It's a school night." He was still facing the computer.

I poked Nils in the shoulder and called back to Jeff, "I have an open period first thing tomorrow. I don't have to be at school until nine!"

Jeff swung around in his chair. "Holly, don't make me be the bad guy. Nine a.m. isn't exactly noon."

"Seriously, though, we'll be fifty feet away from you," Nils continued. "We'll eat a bag of cookies and be asleep by eleven. I just don't want to be alone in my house tonight. So depressing."

"Alone? You don't have parents?"

Nils twisted his body into a pitiable pose—head down, shoulders slumped.

Jeff relented. "Fine, what do I care? You're the ones who're going to pay tomorrow." He walked toward us. "Such a pushover." He kissed my head, then moved past me, walking back down the hall to his bedroom. "I'm taking a shower. If I don't see you guys, have fun. Holly, check in with me in the morning before you leave."

I nodded, did a little jig, then soaped up another greasy dish.

So Nils was the one who supplied the Kahlúa—the only thing he didn't think his parents would notice missing from their liquor cabinet. I scammed two beers out of the fridge in our garage, which we drank while singing along to Billy Joel's "Vienna."

An hour or so later we were drunk. Most of the Kahlúa was gone, both beers were empty, and a large pile of silver Hershey's Kiss wrappers was mounting on the futon between us.

"Okay, so wait, so you go, 'I'm just not ready to be in a committed relationship,' and then she was, like, *what?* She said *what*, exactly??" I was cracking up. Hysterical. Not that Nils and Nora's breakup was even remotely funny.

"And then she was, like, *sad*, Holly. She was sad! Stop laughing! It sucked. I don't like hurting people. Especially not her, she's sweet." He stuffed a handful of chocolate into his mouth.

I swallowed and continued. "No, but seriously, you're right. It *is* sad. It's really sad." I tried twisting my lips into a frown.

"What're you doing to your face right now?"

"I'm frowning."

Nils reached out and touched my mouth. "You're not frowning, Hols, you're, like, smiling but the sides of your lips are turned down."

I tried sitting up but then Nils pulled me back down.

"What time is it?" I asked.

Nils checked his watch. "One."

"Tomorrow's gonna suck, huh?"

Nils reached over and grabbed me by my T-shirt.

"What're you doing?"

"Nothing." He pulled his hand back.

Neither one of us said anything for a second or two. I rolled onto my back, simultaneously sliding a hand down the side of my breast. No lumps. "Hey, Nils?"

"Yeah."

"Do you think cancer is contagious?"

He gave me a quick shove. "You're on drugs."

I looked up. "No, not drugs. *Kahlúa*."

We both broke into hysterics. He reached over and tugged on my T-shirt.

"What're you doing?" I asked again.

"I'm pulling you closer." He yanked hard on the thin cotton. I just lay there, not moving. Laughing.

"Holly, come on. Come closer."

I scooched closer, knocking into the pile of silver wrappers. "Okay," I said. "Here I am."

"Okay, good." Nils repositioned himself so that his body mirrored my body. We both lay on our sides, our knees touching. I was giggling still, saying, "Okay, good," over and over—mimicking his voice, which is deeper than mine. Not *deep* deep. But deeper.

Nils had stopped laughing now and was rubbing the edge of my T-shirt sleeve between two fingers.

"You wanna play Scrabble?" I asked, propping myself up on one elbow.

He shrugged. And then he kissed me. It was a real kiss. With open mouths and tongues and he tasted like cheap chocolate and I liked it. I liked it better than kissing Paul.

I pulled back and he looked at me. I tried picturing Nils and me at the beach, in the backseat of Paul's car. Then I tried picturing us together in my bed. I wanted to laugh. But then he kissed me again. He put his hands on my face and I tugged gently at the belt loop on his jeans before sliding a hand around his waist and pulling him into me. It didn't feel anything like being with Paul. "Nils?"

"Yeah?"

I wasn't sure what I meant to say, so I didn't say anything at all.

And then we kissed again. We kissed for a while and didn't do anything else and then sometime around two thirty, we fell asleep.

Nils had set the alarm on his cell phone to go off at eight a.m. So at eight, a blaring ring sounded. I bolted upright. I was still wearing my clothes from the night before. I picked sleep from my eyes. My head felt like it was about to explode.

"Hey," said Nils, stretching his arms overhead. Then, *"Christ."*

"I can't go to school," I cried, gripping my pulsating head. "I can't do it."

Nils slowly got up on his knees. "You have to, Holly. Jeff'll never let us sleep out here again." He grabbed my arm. "Come on. Get up. Go back to the house. Go take a shower. And drink water. You'll feel better."

I stood up. We both did. Nils grabbed the beer bottles and the empty bottle of Kahlúa and stuffed them into a paper shopping bag we had stashed away in the corner. "I'll dispose of these," he said, lifting the bag.

I walked toward the door and then turned back around. "Last night?"

Nils nodded, looking sheepish. "Yeah."

"Did you . . ." I took a breath. ". . . did you mean to do what you did?"

He scratched his chin, grinning.

I shuffled backward, knocking into the wall on my way to the door. "Ow!" I grabbed my head.

"Watch it, twinkle toes."

"Har, har." I stepped outside, shielding my eyes from the sun with one hand. "See you when I see you," I said, blowing a kiss. Walking back across the lawn toward my house, still drunk.

Chapter 31

English Lit. Kiminski was ranting about *Beowulf*. *Grendel, pagan themes, blah blah*. I couldn't understand a word he was saying. I raised my hand. "Can I go to the bathroom, please?"

"I don't know. *Can* you?" Such an asshole. This was his favorite game. *Grammar time*.

I took a breath, then rephrased the question. "*May* I go to the bathroom?"

"You *may*." And then, under his breath, "For the second time in the last hour . . ."

"Thanks much," I sneered, standing up and walking toward the exit.

I'd kissed Nils. *Kissed NILS*. And the day after tomorrow, Friday, was D-day. When I'd either convince Paul to keep his mouth shut, or he'd blow my life to smithereens. Saskia would hate me. I'd hate me. The *world* would hate me.

Hovering over the toilet bowl, I thought maybe I could make myself puke. My stomach had been somersaulting since second period. I stuck a finger down my throat and gagged. My eyes went watery. No luck. Then I heard some rustling around in the stall next door. The rolling of toilet paper, some sniffling. I looked down and recognized those shoes. Pink leather mules. Ugly. Cheap looking. Probably cost four hundred bucks. "Nora," I said cautiously, "is that you?"

"Who is it?" Her voice cracked. She'd been crying.

"It's Holly."

I heard her undo the latch on her stall, so I did the same. We met by the sinks.

"Hi," she said. She looked horrible. She was wearing a tight pink dress to match her ugly pink shoes, as if she'd really tried to pull it together that morning. Splotches of mascara marked her cheeks.

"Are you okay?" I asked. She was clutching a balled-up wad of toilet paper to her nose.

"You've probably heard. He told you, right?"

I nodded.

"Such an idiot. I didn't even see it coming. How is that possible?"

I didn't know how to comfort her. Under normal circumstances this would have been uncomfortable, but after the night I'd had with Nils . . . ? My stomach rolled over.

Nora let out a sob. "I really liked him, you know? I don't know where to stick all my feelings now. They're still there, just, *torturing* me." Tears shot down her cheeks.

I willed myself to go to her, hug her, *anything* to get the tears to stop, but I couldn't make my legs move. "Can I do anything?" I asked.

"Like what?" She looked genuinely perplexed by my offer to help.

I shrugged. "I dunno. You want a soda from the machine?"

She blew her nose. "Could you talk to him, Holly? Maybe you could find out what I did wrong?"

This crushed me. She was making me so sad. "I don't think . . . I mean, I don't know if it's the best thing, for me to get between you guys."

Nora walked over to the sink. She cupped her hands underneath the faucet and splashed water under her eyes. "Are you sick?" she asked.

"No, why?"

"I heard you gag before I knew it was you."

"Oh . . . my period," I said, quickly covering. "Always makes me wanna hurl."

She considered herself in the mirror, blotting her face with a paper towel. "Do I look okay?"

"You look great," I lied.

She turned toward me. "So is that it? Nils and me? Like, you think it's over for good?" Her eyes were really big. She expected so much.

I shrugged and watched her whole body deflate.

"Thanks, Holly."

"Sure."

She passed me, grabbing my arm on her way out. "Hope your stomach feels better."

"Thanks,"

I locked myself back in the bathroom stall.

Lunch outside on the grass with Saskia. No sandwiches. French fries and fried eggs from the cafeteria.

"You know there's a bonfire Friday night at the beach?"

"Really?" I stuffed four fries into my mouth, chewed quickly, and swallowed. "Who's going?"

"Everyone. I don't even know who's organizing. Should be fun, though." She took a bite of salad. "You'll come, right?"

The thought of another night out with Paul was terrifying to me. Besides, Friday would be exactly one week since we'd last spoken. So we were due. "Maybe," I said. "I dunno, not exactly in the partying mood . . ."

She kicked my leg. "Come on. This is *it*. After this year,

no more bonfires . . . good-bye, Topanga . . . you know? You *have* to come."

I took a long chug of my water bottle. "We'll see."

And then it happened. I suppose it was inevitable. Just a matter of time before Paul, Saskia, and myself all stood face-to-face. We were on the ground, she and I. And then all of a sudden there he was, hovering overhead.

"Babe."

We both looked up. My whole body went rigid. I waited for him to say something shitty.

"Hey!" she squealed, reaching up and grabbing his hands. "Sit!" She patted the grass. "You want fries?"

Paul looked at me. "That's okay. I'm gonna eat inside with Pete and Broder."

Saskia swallowed a big gulp of Coke and threw her hands in the air. "I'm sorry, so rude. Do you two even know each other?"

"Not really," Paul said, real quick, extending a hand for me to shake. "I mean, I know you, but I don't know you."

I took his hand. It was limp.

"Paul, Holly, Holly, Paul."

Paul nodded and squatted down next to Saskia. "I'm going," he said. Then he pulled her forward, leading her by the chin with one hand into a kiss. It was a long kiss, fifteen seconds long—I swear it. At one point he totally opened his eyes and looked at me sideways, just to make sure I'd been watching. I had.

"Really nice meeting you Holly." Paul waved lamely and headed back toward the cafeteria. Saskia looked a little dazed. "What the F? That kiss? Totally for your benefit. He never kisses me like that anymore." She leaned into me. "Hang out more often. Please."

I took a huge bite of cold fried egg.

Chapter 32

So I went to the bonfire. I wasn't going to go but then Nils wanted to go. "Hols, it'll be fun," he'd said, giving me a similar pitch to the one Saskia had thrown at me earlier: *Good-bye Topanga hello big world. Let's go let's go let's go.* So I let him talk me into it. I let him kiss me and promise me nice times. I told myself that Paul had been bluffing and drunk the week before, and that tonight would be just another party at the beach. Bonfires and beer. *No big deal,* I said to myself.

So Nils drove. Nils barely ever drove, but that night he did. We took his dad's truck and parked in the same parking lot that Paul and I had been to a few times, and right before we got out of the car, Nils kissed me. He slid across the seat of his dad's pickup and pulled me into his lap.

He touched my face with his hands and pressed his lips to my lips. He said, "I like it like this. You and I like this together." My stomach went warm. Then we got out of the car. We followed a trail of smoke toward the party. A cluster of kids were huddled together in sweatshirts drinking who-knows-what out of sippy cups in front of the fire. I spotted Nora. Then Paul and Saskia, soon after that.

"Drinks?" I asked Nils, squeezing his hand and heading off in search of beer.

"Drinks." He nodded. Following close behind.

We grabbed two Tecate cans out of a small red cooler by the fire. We drank those, side by side, sitting in a chilly little spot in the sand. Nils made circles on my ankle under my jeans with his pinkie finger. We drank two more Tecates. We watched the others drink and talk and dance and kiss, then we drank another two beers and *presto—chango*! Like magic, we were drunk.

From this point on, things get kind of patchy. I drank a lot, Nils drank a lot, and I can't remember much about the night other than how we all ended up in the end. Here's what I do remember:

Sometime around ten, a crying, drunken Nora pulled Nils away toward the ocean. They sat on a rock and I sat on another rock, alone, until Saskia came by with more beers. We drank those. We danced around the fire. I watched Paul watch me and periodically I would turn backward and watch Nils and Nora but I didn't care much about anything. I wanted to dance. I danced and danced and sometime around midnight Nils came over and said, "I'm fucked, Nora's driving me crazy. I'm gonna go sleep in the car." And I said okay. And then I can't remember how much time lapsed but suddenly Saskia was gone, most of the party was gone, and I'd been asleep on a towel for hours. Paul woke me up.

"Time to go, Holly."

"Hmm?" I was half asleep still. I sat up, spinning.

"I'm gonna drive you home, okay?"

I let him take my hand. We stood up. "What about Nils?" I asked. "Where's Nils?"

"He left," Paul said. And that was that.

We ended up back at The Shack. I don't know how. I don't know if I told him to take me there or what. Maybe I thought I'd wait there for Nils. I don't really know now. All I know is there we were, Paul and I, and it was dark and I was drunk, and I let him undress me. I let him take all my clothes off and kiss me and it's not like I told him no or anything, I was into it. I remember that part. I remember undoing the buckle on his pants and I remember that he kept his shirt and his shoes on. I can't tell you why I did what I did. All I know is hours later, when I woke up alone with my pants in a ball on the floor by the futon, I wanted to die. It was light out and I was halfway sober and I knew

Lauren Strasnick

what I'd done and felt nothing but shame. I opened my mouth to cry but no sound came out and then I pulled my underwear back on and picked my jeans up off the ground. I got dressed and walked back to the house.

Chapter 33

In my dream, Mom was my age and wearing that gauzy cotton dress of hers I wore the first time I went hiking with Paul. Ballanoff was there too, dressed up in that stupid fuzzy cardigan he's always wearing in the auditorium on really cold days. Mom was kissing Ballanoff, only *I* was the one feeling the kisses—soft and exhilarating and similar to how it felt kissing Nils in The Shack that one night. Mom had her arms wrapped around the back of Ballanoff's head and his hands were gripping her waist. Jeff was there too, as were Nils and Paul and Mom's old boyfriend Michael. They were all there, watching from the sidelines as if kissing were a spectator sport. Like tennis. Or golf.

But then Mom was alone. No Ballanoff or Jeff. Mom was alone and all the love I'd felt between her and Ballanoff had vanished. Then the room changed shades. It went from dark to light, then from light to white, and Mom was suddenly see-through, drifting up and away, dissolving into the clean white walls, fading like a soft stain or an old photograph.

Chapter 34

I sat in front of the TV and tried to watch something about bowhead whales on the Discovery Channel but couldn't focus. I just sat there watching the screen lights blink and tried to keep myself from crying. Harry hugged my ankles while I thought about Nils and Saskia and how I could never take back what I'd done. Then I heard a rattling at the front door and didn't turn around because I figured it was Jeff, who'd been out in the yard all morning planting annuals.

"You're here. What happened to you last night?"

It was Nils. My fingers went tingly. I twisted around so I could see him. He looked adorable. His hair was all mussed from sleep. Looking at him made my heart hurt. "Hey." I stood up. "I'm here, yeah, I'm fine. Saskia drove me home," I lied. "Someone said you'd left and I was so messed up, Nils, I couldn't even walk straight. . . ."

He moved toward me. "I woke up at, like, five thirty, in the backseat of the pickup and I was still at the beach. And I couldn't find you and I flipped." Now we were hugging. He'd buried his face in my neck and was kissing me. "You smell so clean," he said, running a hand through my wet hair.

"I just showered."

"You feel nice," he said, rocking me from side to side. "I was so scared, I thought something really bad had happened."

I felt a tear trickle down my cheek. *Tell him,* I thought. *Tell him tell him tell him what you've done.* I wiped my eyes and pulled backward so we were face-to-face.

"Are you crying?" he asked, scrunching his brow.

I opened my mouth to say it. *I'm a horrible person,* I thought. *I don't deserve you,* I thought. And then my cell rang. Nils dropped his arms to his sides and I stepped forward to check the caller ID screen on my phone. It was Saskia. *Saskia.* I turned to Nils, and my face must have looked really weird because he said, "What's wrong with you? Who's calling?"

I just stood there and thought, *Saskia knows. Soon Nils will know too. Tell him, Holly, before he finds out some other way.* But I couldn't do it. I wanted to have him for as long as I could have him before he realized what a horrible person I was. "No one. I'm just so tired. Come sleep with me?" I took him by the hand and led him down the hall toward my room. "Let's just get into bed and sleep for a while? I'm so tired," I said.

So that's what we did. We kicked off our shoes and crawled into bed together and then we just slept. Side by side, Nils's body curled around my body from behind.

When I woke up around five, it was already almost dark out. Nils was gone. I checked my phone. Three new messages. I didn't check my call log to see who they were from. Instead, I dropped my phone back on my bed and shuffled in my socks down the hall to the kitchen. There was a note from Jeff on the fridge that he'd gone to the store. Harry was with him. I sat back down on the couch and turned on the TV. I watched the last half of *Agnes of God* on Showtime, then grabbed my book off the coffee table and headed out back to The Shack to read.

The lights were already on inside. I could see a thin line of soft yellow creeping out from beneath the old, tin door. I pressed my book to my chest and went inside. There was Nils, sitting on the futon with his head down. Clutching something little and plastic and blue.

"Hi," I said. "You left. Where'd you go?"

He held the little plastic thing up high above his head. "I came out here, to read. This was on the bed." It was a condom wrapper. *A condom wrapper.* I hadn't even checked The Shack when I'd left that morning. *Stupid stupid stupid, Holly.* I looked down at Nils and plucked the little plastic wrapper from his fingertips. I felt like someone had socked me in the chest.

"You wanna tell me what that's about?" he said. He was still looking at the ground.

"It's . . . mine, I guess." I sat down next to him. I put my hand on his shoulder. He shrugged it off. "Will you look at me, please? I have something to tell you."

"I don't want to look at you."

My eyes blurred. *This is it,* I thought. *Six years of friendship, wrecked in a blink.* "I didn't mean to do it. I can't even remember half the night, Nils. . . ."

He moved away from me. His head was still down.

"Can you look at me? Please?"

He shook his head. He said, "The thing is, it's not that you were with someone else, even though that kills me. Because it's not like we had a title. It's not like we were committed or anything." He laughed but it sounded so sad, his laugh. "The thing that makes it bad is that you brought him *here.* And this is *our* place. And you *promised.*"

I wanted to die. He was right. What's worse than a broken promise?

"Who was it?" he asked, biting his thumb. "Not that it matters. But I'd kind of like to know. Is it that same guy you just ended stuff with?" He glanced over at me. I nodded.

"So? Who is he? Do I know him?"

I nodded again and bit the insides of my cheeks. "Paul Bennett," I said, looking down at my lap.

Nils exhaled. "You're really something, Holly."

"I know," I said, tears burning my cheeks.

"Paul Bennett."

"Yeah."

"Paul Bennett? Holly, I hate that guy."

"I know."

"That guy's a total asshole—"

"He is."

"And he has a girlfriend."

"I know . . ."

"She's your *friend*, right? Ever since Stein's class, you guys have been, like, *madly* in love, right?"

"Sort of. Yes," I said softly.

His face was red. He looked at me and I made myself hold his gaze. "Where's your *heart*? How could you do that to someone you care about?"

"I don't know. I'm horrible. I told you, I'm awful, remember?" I clutched his arm. "But you promised you'd always be my friend. You swore it."

He looked at my hand on his arm. "Please, don't touch me."

I let out a cry and pulled back. I dropped my head to my lap and shook. Tears soaking the knees of my jeans.

Nils stood up. "I feel sorry for you."

I continued to cry.

"Really, you're just . . . pathetic," he said, pushing past me.

I heard the door swing shut and felt my heart split in two.

Sunday night I finally checked my voice mail. Three messages from Saskia, each of them hang ups. One was from Paul: "Hi. She knows. For the record, it wasn't me who told her. Sarah Wehle saw us leave together Friday night." Click. Sarah *Wehle*, of course. I could never remember that girl's last name.

I thought about staying home Monday, but I figured eventually I'd have to go back and face everyone. I hadn't spoken to Nils since Saturday night in The Shack. I hadn't called Saskia or Paul back. So this was my shining debut. My big day back.

I got up that morning and put on a clean shirt and a pair of jeans I hadn't washed in three weeks. I put kibble in Harry's bowl and scratched behind his ears like I did every morning before I left for school. I got in my car and didn't turn on the radio. I drove and I drove and then I parked in my usual spot and just sat there, my car idle. I stared at the soccer field. It was seven forty. Time to face the execution squad.

At first, everything seemed pretty status quo. Same kids, same corridor, just another miserable Monday morning,

Nothing Like You

175

everyone sleepy-eyed and slurping out of enormous paper coffee cups. Then I spotted Paul dumping a pile of books into his locker. Then Saskia down at the end of the hall, surrounded by a group of blondes in peasant blouses with designer stitching on the butts of their jeans. They didn't notice me at first, I skated past their group and nobody seemed to see me until I reached my locker. There, in pretty purple cursive, the word "whore" marked my door. Perfect penmanship. Someone had really taken the time to make that awful word look gorgeous.

Here's the weird thing. I didn't feel anything. Not sad, not guilty really, I felt as if I were hovering outside my own body, watching the whole sorry scene unfold in slow-mo on primetime TV. I can only liken the feeling to my mother's memorial, where I felt like the lead character in a Lifetime movie about motherless daughters. I'd drifted down that auditorium aisle toward the life-size ugly poster board picture of Mom at the beach, and there was Jeff, at my side. Dozens of grief-washed faces watching us walk. *Poor little girl,* I heard them thinking, *poor motherless Holly.* Me, though, I hadn't felt a thing. This was the same, only different. This was no pity party. *Persecution* party, maybe. Which sounds so dramatic, because really, I'm no victim. I'm the villain here.

I undid the combo lock on my locker and unloaded the contents of my book bag, leaving only my World History text and a spiral notebook for next class. That's when I heard a soft, raspy echoing. A singsongy chorus. "Holly Whore," they sang, over and over. I spun the lock on my locker and started back down the hall toward class. I hummed a few bars from "Holly Holy" softly to myself, trying to drown out their voices. Then the chanting died down. I heard a couple of kids laugh. Someone threw something at my head. A balled-up piece of paper, maybe? It was light, I don't know. I didn't turn around to look.

Saskia wasn't in World History even though I'd seen her in the hallway that morning. I went through all four periods before lunch feeling perfectly, contentedly numb. Then, on my walk out to the back patio with my brown bag at lunch, Nils came careening around the side of the building. We collided, knocking heads. Then quickly, without warning, I was weeping. Hysterical. My body folded over. I clutched my stomach, trying to catch my breath. Nils took me by the arm and led me around the bend to a private little grassy patch by the science wing.

"Holly, stop it." He held me at arm's length by my shoulders. "Seriously, stop crying. You have to stop. You're making a scene."

I stood up a little, nodded, and held my breath. "I was fine all morning," I huffed. "I couldn't feel a thing."

Nils sat down on the ground and pulled me down next to him. "I saw your locker."

I nodded.

"Holly . . . *why?*"

I bit my lip. "I don't know. I liked him. It sounds so stupid, but I actually thought he cared about me. And then I met *her* and I ended things. And he got so mad. And then stuff started happening with you, and I don't know. I don't know why I did what I did." I looked at him. "I really don't."

Nils stuck his thumbnail in his mouth and bit down. "Just . . . why'd you have to go and wreck everything?"

I shrugged. "This is, like, my worst nightmare. You know that, right? The whole world could hate me, I wouldn't care . . . but you? I can't handle you hating me, Nils."

He looked down at the ground and pulled at a patch of grass. "Did it mean anything to you? The other night? With me, in The Shack?"

I leaned forward and grabbed his hand. "It meant *everything* to me."

He snapped his hand back and stood up abruptly. "I'm sorry." He shook his head. "I'm sorry about your locker, Holly. I feel bad for you, I do. But I can't see you for a while, okay?"

I nodded, my chest tightening.

"You should talk to Saskia," he said, readjusting his backpack. "You should tell her you're sorry."

I shook my head. "I can't even look at her. I can't even be in the same room as her."

"I saw her on the lawn by the auditorium before I saw you. She's alone down there, Holly. You should go."

So I went. I went because Nils told me to go.

She was lying on her back in the grass in the sun. I was about to ruin everything.

"Hi," I croaked. I was standing over her now.

She blinked her eyes at me. She said, "I called you three times this weekend." I don't know what I'd been expecting. Hysterics? A beating? I'm not sure what. I just didn't expect her to seem so cool and together.

"I know."

She propped herself up on her elbows and looked at me. "Are you going to sit down or no?"

I dropped down on my knees next to her. She looked at me and I looked down at the ground. "I'm so sorry," I said.

"Oh yeah? For what?"

"For . . ." I took a breath. She was going to make me say it.

"What's wrong, Holly? What're you sorry for?" She was staring into me. Her expression was blank.

I looked to my right, at a cluster of her friends watching us from the patio. "I'm so sorry . . . for what happened between Paul and me."

"Right." She shrugged. "So, like, what specifically happened that you're so sorry for?"

My stomach lurched. I deserved this. I did what I did. I should be able to say it out loud to Saskia's face. "For being with him," I whispered, closing my eyes.

"Could you look at me, please?"

My eyes fluttered open. I looked at her.

"So . . . you're sorry for screwing my boyfriend? That's what you're saying?"

I thought I might hurl. I nodded.

She got up on her knees and picked up her book bag. "Well, I don't accept your apology."

I felt the familiar sting of tears, then watched as she walked across the lawn and back toward her friends. One of them flipped me off.

Paul was waiting for me outside by my car after school. He was leaning against my driver side door, smoking a cigarette.

I scowled. "Move, please? I wanna go home."

"Exhausting day, huh?"

I mashed my lips together and stared at him. He was still leaning against my car door. "Move. Please."

He took a drag and slowly stepped away. I stuck my key in the lock.

"For the record," he said, "I wasn't planning on telling her. I mean, had she not asked . . ."

I turned around to face him. "You said—I mean you basically told me flat out last week you were gonna tell her if I didn't keep having sex with you."

"I was drunk. I didn't mean it." He softened a little. "She asked me what was going on. I couldn't lie."

I rolled my eyes. "Sure, you could've. You've been doing it all year long."

"Well, look at it this way: It's all out there now. No guilt." He touched my waist. "Nothing to feel bad about anymore . . ."

"You wrecked my life."

He grimaced. "*You* wrecked your life. I didn't hold a gun to your head. I didn't make you *do* anything."

"You took advantage."

"*Take. Responsibility. Holly.*" He leaned into me. "I didn't. Have sex. With myself." His arms were resting against the hood of the car, locking me in on both sides of my body. I heard the door handle pop. He pulled open my car door, bumping my butt forward. I jumped.

"How're things between you and your little boyfriend? By the way."

I threw my book bag across the seat and got into my car. I kept one foot on the pavement. "You feel good about yourself when you go to sleep at night?"

Paul shrugged.

"Yeah. Me neither." I slammed my car door shut.

Chapter 35

Nils had gone to Hawaii with his family for the holidays. I spent my break watching the wall. Hiking with Harry. Watching TV. Doing macramé.

Sometime around day nine I was sprawled out on the carpet of my bedroom floor, listening to Mom's Neil Diamond CDs, searching for something to occupy my mind, when I saw something white-ish and square underneath the bed. I pinched it between my fingertips. It was Frank Gellar's card.

I have nothing, I thought. *No friends. No mom. I have this, though.* I grabbed my cell out of my bag and dialed.

He picked up. "Hello?"

"Is this Frank?"

"Yes."

"This is Holly Hirsh."

"I remember you. You're the girl who cancelled on me. Twice."

I winced. "I know. I'm sorry."

"Don't tell me. You're finally ready to reschedule."

"I promise to show up."

"It's ninety for the half hour. You don't give me a twenty-four-hour head's up before canceling this time, I have to charge you, anyway."

"I understand. And I won't cancel this time. I swear it."

Frank Gellar's place was small and brown. Lots of dark wood, lots of furniture. The tabletops were cluttered with trinkets and crystals and the shelves were stacked with books on spiritual this and metaphysical that. I waited in the living room while he puttered around his office, arranging things. "Holly, you want to tape the session?" He held up an ancient recorder. "Okay." I nodded, standing up.

"Come on in," he said, waving me forward with both hands.

I took a seat on the dingy cream-colored couch in the corner. Frank sat down in an overstuffed green chair a few feet away. He was a big man, middle-aged, with a white beard and a bland, friendly face. He looked a lot like how I thought god might look to a kid. Minus the ponytail and the green khaki shorts.

"So, I'm just going to ask you to take a few deep breaths." He pushed the red button on the tape recorder.

I nodded and inhaled a couple of times in a row.

"Don't forget to exhale. Breathe."

I giggled nervously. I tried again. *Inhale, exhale.*

"Good." He closed his eyes and took a raspy, loud breath. Then he didn't do anything for a little bit. He just breathed with his eyes shut. I watched him, halfway expecting he'd start talking in tongues, but after a minute or so he just looked at me and said, "Yes and no answers only, okay?

I nodded.

"Keep yourself open. You may have someone specific you're hoping to hear from, but someone else might come through with a message instead."

"Okay," I said. "Wait, though. Wait?"

He looked up.

"I don't want to be told anything bad. Like, when I'm going to die or anything. Can you not tell me that kind of stuff?"

"This isn't that sort of reading. I promise. Nothing bad, okay?"

I relaxed a little.

Frank took a few more breaths, then started with, "I'm getting the letter *A*." He said it sounded like an *A*, like the name *Anne* or *Annie* and did that make sense to me? And yes, it made sense. Mom's mom's name was Anna, and she'd died the year before Mom from a stroke in the tub.

"The *A* name has a male *K* with her. A contemporary. Meaning a brother or a husband or a friend." Quite possible, since my grandmother had eight siblings, but I'd only known one: Auntie Jean, who'd died when I was eight from a massive coronary. She'd been alone at the time. My grandmother had found her on the floor clutching a rolling pin.

I didn't know any *K*s, though.

"There's a cancer death," he said next. My heart sped up. I leaned forward, put my hands on my thighs, and said, "That's right, yeah, cancer." And then he said Mom's name. Well, not her name, exactly. At first he just said, "Bear."

"That's close," I whispered. And he went on to say it two or three different ways as if he'd heard it wrong the first time. Then, finally, after a few deep breaths—a few eye blinks and cracked knuckles—he said *Barrett*. Mom's name. *Barrett*. I got teary and hot. Which is so embarrassing, crying in front of a complete stranger—a middle-aged man with a beard, no less—but that's the way it happened, so *hey*.

"Here," he said, handing me a tissue. Then, "Look, she's telling me to bring up the dog."

Harry. *Harry.* I grabbed another tissue from the Kleenex box and pressed it to the corner of one eye. Frank looked at me blankly and took another breath. This was the last thing he said: "You are very loved." He raised a glass of water to his skinny lips, hidden beneath acres of scruffy beard. "You need to work harder at loving yourself."

Chapter 36

Amazing, what you can grow used to.

"You can't eat that in here, you know that, right?"

February, and I'd finally acclimated to all the shittiness at school. At long last I'd worked out the perfect system for keeping myself invisible: open blocks on the back patio, lunches in the library stacks, reading cheesy mystery novels.

"Eat what?" I asked, my mouth full, shoving my sandwich behind my back, covering my face with the paperback I'd been reading.

"Come on, Holly. No food allowed. You know that." Ms. McGovern was standing over me, clicking a pencil against her top two teeth. "Take that out to the cafeteria."

"No, look, I'm done," I said, swallowing, then rewrapping my sandwich and shoving it back in my bag. "No more eating, I swear. Just reading." I flashed a smile and waved my book around overhead. McGovern tugged on the waistband of her rayon slacks, then backed away, leaving me to my books and solitude. I made sure she'd returned to her station at the circulation desk before getting up and moving farther back, to another spot by the computer lab that seemed much more secluded.

I dumped my things in a pile by the printer and relaxed back against the leg of one of the vacant desks. I opened my book back up. I took my sandwich back out of my bag.

Kneeling in the hallway, fishing through my bag for a tube of lipstick or a pen or maybe my new book, I spotted Saskia. She was just a few yards off, leaning against her locker, talking to Sarah Wehle, who was doing some sort of animated song and dance, trying to elicit a happy reaction from Saskia, who just looked so sad, standing there, chewing her sandy blond hair. We hadn't spoken since December. I felt a sick pang in my gut, then sprang to my feet, rushing forward. I was going to make a move. I was going to *say something. I can undo this,* I thought. *I can make everything better.*

But as I got more near, Sarah's eyes were suddenly on me, narrowing. Soon after, Saskia and I were locked in a stare-off. I froze, midstep, watching them watch me. My impulse to say something, to make some big overture or gesture, instantly faded. I turned a quick pivot, then walked swiftly in the opposite direction. *What could I possibly say now, anyways?* Everything had already been said.

Nils was ten yards away, approaching fast.

"You look good," I said. These, the first words we'd exchanged since he'd gotten back from his trip, in early January.

"Thanks," he whispered, smiling tightly, passing me quickly in the hallway on his walk to the auditorium.

He was taking a class with Ballanoff this quarter. I'd done some investigative work and discovered this. I loved the idea of Nils doing those weirdo acting warm-ups alongside Ballanoff. Somehow, it kept me feeling connected to him, still.

And he did look good. His hair looked longer, like he hadn't bothered with a cut in the last month or two. *Maybe the new girlfriend likes it long,* I thought. New girlfriend. *Barf.* Eleanor Bishop. *Hurl.*

They'd been inseparable since January. Typical Nils. Barely a breath between women. But she was smart, Eleanor, nothing like Nora. She wore understated clothes and cared about important things like stray dogs and global warming. I hated her. I hated her small, boyish body and her square black glasses. I hated watching Nils hold her hand in the hall. Sometime, somewhere, I'd heard someone say she was *saving herself*—for what, I'm not sure. But she had principles, was

Nothing Like You

189

the point. She had virtue. Two things I'd had once but had lost along the way.

"Okay, well . . . see you!" I cried insanely, calling after him. He turned awkwardly and nodded a quick "Sure thing" before pushing past the big double doors to the auditorium.

Nora asked me for rides home, still. Once she'd heard that Nils's and my friendship had completely dissolved, she felt bad for me, I think.

"Have you guys talked at all?" she asked.

We were in my car after school driving home. Nora was wearing her favorite oversize sweatshirt and a pair of low-waisted pale jeans.

"Not really. No." She looked so sympathetic. I loathed thinking Nora and I might be feeling something similar. Two peas, same pod, that sort of thing. "What about you?" I asked.

"Same thing." But it wasn't the same. Nils's and Nora's short-lived romance could never compare to the six years I'd spent with him. Not ever.

I smiled and turned up her driveway. "Here you go. Door to door." I pulled the car to a stop.

"You wanna come in?" she asked, unbuckling her seat belt and turning to face me.

I appreciated the invite. I did. She was the one person at

school who was still making an effort, and that meant loads to me. Still . . . "Not today. I have to take Harry out for a run. Thanks, though."

"Okay," she said, stepping out onto the gravel. "It gets easier, you know." She was bending down now, watching me through the open window on the passenger side door.

"Time heals, right?"

She gave a firm nod. "Exactly. All wounds."

Chapter 37

One Saturday morning in early March, I wandered out of my room half asleep and stopped when I heard something coming from inside Jeff and Mom's bedroom. I cracked the door and poked my head inside. Jeff had two huge cardboard boxes on the bed and was weeding through Mom's closet.

"What're you doing?"

"Hols, honey, hi. Come in here, will you? Do you want any of this stuff?"

"What is this?"

"Anything you want, take. The rest of it I think we should just drop off at Goodwill."

I walked forward and sat down on the bed, next to a pile of Mom's dresses. I rubbed some silky material between my fingertips. "You're really getting rid of her stuff?"

Jeff sat back, pushing a chunk of hair off his forehead. "She's not coming back, Hols, you know? What am I going to do with nine hundred dresses and a billion different face creams? Especially with you leaving? I can't hold on to this stuff forever."

"No, I know." I looked down at the silky cream-colored dress I was running back and forth between my fingers. "I want this one, though, okay?"

Jeff nodded. "Of course. Whatever you want."

"Her perfume, too. And just, don't get rid of any of her really old stuff until I get a chance to go through it, okay?"

"Okay." Jeff squeezed my shoulder. Then he turned back toward Mom's closet and pulled out this black puffy number made from velvet and crinoline. The black-tie bar mitzvah dress. Big hit at weddings, too.

"I hated that thing." I sniffed, grabbing the dress by its stiff skirt, walking it over to the full-length mirror and holding it up to my body. "Can I keep it?"

Jeff stood up. "You do this: Whatever you don't want, we'll get rid of." He kissed the top of my head and walked out into the hallway. "I'll make the eggs," he said.

So here's what I ended up with: eleven dresses, some of her nicer shoes, a pair of Pumas she'd never worn (to wear on my hikes, with Harry), her perfumes and a few toiletries that smelled like her soaps, hand lotions, etc. I thought briefly about Mom's cancer again, i.e., *could I catch it?* Then I pushed back that thought and slipped a light blue baggy sweatshirt of hers over my head.

I kept all her jewelry, too. The rest I took to Goodwill.

As I was unloading my boxes out onto the curb, Saskia's car pulled into the open parking spot right next to me. A tall boy with a messy blond mop of hair pushed his way out from her passenger side door. Saskia followed. "Oh. Hi," she said, startled.

"Surprise," I deadpanned, turning back to my boxes.

"Weeding out?"

I whipped around. This was the first time she'd spoken to me in months. "Yeah. Mom's stuff. Jeff finally had me clean out her closets this morning."

Saskia pursed her lips. "We're picking up Thai, for dinner." She gestured to the boy behind her. "This is Sean, by the way."

Her brother. *Oh.*

"Hi," he said, looking at the ground.

"Holly," I whispered. And that's when he looked up. When he heard me say my name.

"Okay, well, we should get going," Saskia slammed her car door shut and the two of them backed their way toward the restaurant next door. I wanted to tell her I missed her. That I was sorry for what I'd done. That knowing her, even briefly, had changed me for the better. Instead, I said, "Yeah, of course. See you around." I picked a box up off the hot cement, carried it ten feet, and dumped it into the donation bin. *Bye-bye, Mom.*

Chapter 38

"What if I went up north, to Santa Cruz? What would you think if I did that?"

Monday night. TV night. Jeff and I were side by side on the couch. It was early April. I'd just gotten three acceptance letters. One rejection.

"I think it'd be great. Is that what you're thinking?"

I shrugged. "Maybe."

He twisted his body sideways so we were facing each other. "Why maybe? You want to stay down here? Go to UCLA?"

"I want to leave. And I don't want to leave."

He put a hand on my head.

"What about you and me?" I asked. "I mean, if I leave, what happens to you and me?"

Jeff muted the television. "Nothing happens to you and me. You're my kid. You'll be five hours north, Hols, no big deal." He cocked his head, holding my gaze. "You worried about me?"

I chewed the inside of my lip and ran the ball of my foot over Harry's head. He was lying on the rug beneath the coffee table.

"Honey, this is your *life*. I'll be fine. I'm a grown man. I want you to do what feels right for you."

I pressed my lips together and felt my eyes start to water. "Okay." I nodded.

"Okay," said Jeff. He slipped his hand around my neck and pulled me into him. I leaned my head against his shoulder and turned the sound back up on the TV. We stayed like that, my head on his shoulder, for a while. At least until the show was over. Maybe even longer.

Chapter 39

The week before graduation I was lying on my back in the stacks at the library, leafing through *Mexican Cooking Made Easy*. It was my free period.

"A real page-turner. Have you gotten to the part about the measuring cup?"

I dropped the book to my chest and looked up. It was Nils. He held his hand out. I grabbed it and let him pull me so I was sitting upright. "Hi," I said.

"Hi." He sat down next to me, dropping two library books and his bag. "I got out of Trig early. Just . . . returning books."

I nodded. We didn't say anything for a little while. I picked at the stiff orange carpeting. "I was looking for recipes for graduation dinner."

"Big party?"

"Me and Jeff, is all."

Nils sucked in his cheeks.

"What about you guys? Plans?"

"Mastro's, I think. Dad wants steak."

I stretched my legs out in front of me. Nils and I were barely an inch apart. "I decided on Santa Cruz," I blurted, tucking some loose hair behind my ear.

"You did? Hols, that's great." He seemed legitimately happy for me. "Jeff's fine with it?"

"He's practically shoving me out the door." I smiled and bit my top lip, sliding my leg closer, so we were touching. "What about you? You know yet?"

Nils nodded. "NYU."

"Oh, Nils. Wow. That's really something."

I felt my throat constrict. It was really happening. We were leaving home. No time to patch things up. A few months and *poof*, we'd both be gone for good.

"I miss you already," I said, looking at him, then quickly darting my eyes down. Nils pressed his foot against my foot.

"How's Eleanor?" I asked, not looking up.

"Eleanor is . . . fine," he said.

"What's gonna happen when you leave?"

"I suppose we'll break up."

"Just like that?"

Nils shrugged.

"Is it serious?" I asked, trying to seem neutral.

"Oh, you know. She's no Holly."

I blinked. Nils was staring straight at me. My stomach rolled over.

"I really do miss you," I said.

"You really hurt me, Holly."

"I know." I leaned forward and grabbed his leg. "Remember in seventh grade when Mom and Jeff took us to the water park and I peed in the wave pool?"

Nils eyed me blankly.

"Remember?"

"Yeah, I remember."

"We've been friends our *whole* lives."

"Not that long . . ."

"Fine, *half* our lives, but what, so that's *it*? We graduate and you go three thousand miles away and then we're just, like, 'bye. Great knowing you. Fun peeing next to you in the wave pool that one time. . . .'"

Nils laughed. I let my head drop back against the book stacks. "You can't be alone, can you?" I said.

He flashed his teeth.

"There's always someone . . . Nora, *me*, Eleanor . . . Kim and what's-her-face—Keri Blumenthal—last year. . . . You have dependency issues."

"I'm a romantic."

"That's one word for it."

We stared at each other for a while. Then Nils pulled his legs to his chest, resting his elbows against his knees. "Fine. But it's not gonna be like it was before. I have a girlfriend now, anyways."

"I know," I said.

"It's not gonna be, like, every night in The Shack or whatever."

I got up on my shins and bounced a little. "No, I *know*."

He pushed his bangs to one side and made his eyes into small slits. "I feel like you manipulated me with that wave pool story. . . ."

I gave him a light shove. The bell rang. Nils stood up and swung his bag across his chest. "So. See you around . . . ?" he asked, sounding unsure.

I righted myself, grabbing the cookbook and my bag. "Hows about 'see you later'?" I said.

Nils nodded and took a step back. I pushed past him, touching his arm on my way to the circulation desk.

Chapter 40

Mom died last spring. A week and a half before she passed, when things started to look especially bad, when just saying hello hurt her, and when taking a trip to the toilet had become a near impossibility, Nils's family, then about to embark on a ten-day trip to Joshua Tree, asked me if I wanted to come away with them.

"What do you think? I shouldn't go, right? Mom seems worse."

Jeff and I were on the porch drinking seltzer. I stuck a finger into my cup and pulled out an ice cube, tossing it onto the lawn.

"No, no, I think you *should* go. What else have you got going on? It'll be nice to get away for a bit."

"You think?" I asked, looking up really quick. "I mean,

you think Mom . . . you think she'll mind?" I asked, pulling a clump of hair to one side and twisting it around my fist.

Jeff picked his cup up off the deck. "Of course Mom won't mind. I think it's a great idea, Hols. Go. Relax for a bit. What's gonna change in ten days?" My eyes shot up toward Jeff. He was staring into his drink, swirling it around and around.

We all knew what might change in ten days. That if I left, I'd possibly come home to *just* Jeff. Mom would be gone.

"Okay, then, I'll tell Nils I can go."

"Good. That'll be good," Jeff said, touching my shoulder, taking a quick sip of seltzer before getting up and heading back in to the house.

Chapter 41

Ballanoff and I sat side by side in the student center on my open block, drinking tepid tea.

"You ready for this?" he asked, staring forward, not even turning to face me.

"Ready for what?"

"Graduation. Growing up. Leaving home?"

"Sure thing," I said, playing with the zipper on my hoodie. Dragging it up and down, *up and down*, making my own pretty rhythm.

"How's Jeff handling you leaving?"

"Good. He's been really good with things. Surprisingly supportive," I said, taking a sip of tea. I wanted to tell Ballanoff that I'd miss him. That he'd made this year bearable. That even though, soon, he'd cease to be my teacher, I still wanted to know him. Instead I said, "What're you doing with your break this summer?"

"Renovating. Nancy wants another office. So we're knocking down one wall and building another." He looked at me. Then he turned back to his bottle.

"Can I ask you something?" I said, watching his profile, wondering what kind of dad he might have been, if things would have gone differently, if Mom might still be around had Ballanoff and Mom dated longer, loved each other, gotten married.

"Yeah, yeah," he said, meeting my gaze.

"You really think I'm that much like her? I mean, when she was my age? Are we really that much the same?"

Ballanoff shook his head. "You're your own person, Holly. I mean, sure, you look like her, but you're *not* her, you're *you*."

I nodded, grateful. "I wish it made me happy, hearing I look like her. I used to really love it, you know? Before she got sick?"

He dropped his bottle and scooched his chair back so we were facing each other. "You're *you*," he said. "You know, your mom made certain choices that I can pretty much guarantee, if faced with a similar crossroads, you wouldn't have made."

I nodded.

"Her path . . . that's not yours to follow. Okay?"

I resisted the urge to cry.

"Worst-case scenario, you face something similar . . . you fight, right?" He looked at me sympathetically. "Hey, you're your own person."

I swiped a hand over one wet cheek. We locked eyes.

"Besides, your mom? *Much* friendlier, much less *sass*." Ballanoff scrunched up his nose, smiling wryly.

I laughed, *relieved* to be laughing, using a napkin off the table to blow my nose. "You always know the right thing to say."

"I do, right? Ballanoff nudged my arm softly. "I totally do."

Chapter 42

It's August and I'm on my way up north, to school. An hour ago I loaded the last box into my backseat and said good-bye to Jeff and Harry. I cried and Jeff cried and Harry licked my cheeks and my ears. Nils came by with mixes. Two for the road. The one he told me to play first, I'm listening to right now. "Aqualung," "Vienna," "Dust in the Wind." All Mom's favorites.

"I'll call you when I get to New York," he said. Jeff and Harry had gone inside and Nils and I were standing in my driveway, leaning against my car door looking grim.

"Okay." I tucked a longish chunk of wayward hair behind one ear. I looked at the ground.

My summer had ended up being better than I'd expected: lots of reading and packing and beach-time and Jeff-time.

Harry had turned four. Nils and I had somehow managed to make the past the past and our friendship was just now starting to look pretty close to how it had looked pre-Holly-senior-year-mental-breakdown.

"We could write letters?" I suggested.

"You won't write me actual letters."

"I will!"

"Actual letters? On paper with pen?"

"Actual letters," I said firmly, nodding my head and catching his eye. He looked so squinty and sad. I was certain I looked the same.

"Well . . ." I checked my watch. It was eleven. I needed to be up at school by five. "Time to go," I said, opening my arms extra wide.

"What's that for?" Nils asked, batting at my arms.

"You're not gonna hug me good-bye?"

"Holly." He stepped forward and slipped his hands around my waist. He pulled me closer, tighter, until we were locked in a snug embrace. "Don't go," he whispered.

I dug my chin into his bony shoulder. "Okay," I said, pulling back a bit, then mashing my forehead against his forehead. "Screw college! I'll stay right here forever."

He exhaled and I could feel his breath on my face. I shut my eyes.

Nils and Eleanor are still together. She's going to Brown in Rhode Island, a four-hour drive from Manhattan, so she and

Nils are gonna give the whole long-distance thing a whirl.

"Hols?"

"Hmm?"

. . . I give it three months. *Tops.*

"Come closer."

We were staring. *Staring staring* with our heads stuck together and then Nils pressed his nose to my nose and I reached up and put both hands on his face. The air smelled like grass and exhaust and it was sunny out, it's *always* sunny, and I wondered for a second if Jeff could see us standing this way—head to head—from the window facing the driveway in our kitchen.

"See you when I see you?" Nils asked, backing away, tugging at a loose thread hanging off the waistband of his jeans.

"See you when I see you," I said, watching him walk backward. Past The Shack, across the lawn, and back to his house on the other side of the stone wall that divides our pretty properties.

I've got four and a half hours till I reach sunny Santa Cruz. I roll down my windows and turn up the volume on my stereo.

The ocean is on my left.

Enormous thanks to Michelle Andelman, for her invaluable
feedback and steadfast belief in this book; to Anica Rissi, for her passion,
enthusiasm, and for loving Holly just as much as I do;
to the entire team at Simon Pulse, for their hard work and support;
and to Jen Rofé, for taking in a stray.

Thank you Adeline Colangelo, for early encouragement;
Jordan Press, for keeping the faith; and Alisa Libby, for leading the way.

Lovely ladies of Juniper Lake: Amanda Yates, Milly Sanders, Margaret
Wappler, Anna Spanos, Justine Schroeder Garrett, and Jenna Blough.
You make life better. I love you all.

Thank you Jade Chang and Bruce Bauman.

Lastly, endless thanks go to my father,
Ken Strasnick, for being the most awesome dad around;
and to my brother, Aaron: you fifty-pound miracle, you.

Lauren Strasnick grew up in Greenwich, Connecticut, now lives in Los Angeles, California, and is a graduate of Emerson College and the California Institute of the Arts MFA Writing Program. She wrote her first short story, "Yours Truly, the Girls from Bunk Six" in a cloth-bound 5x4 journal, in fifth grade. *Nothing Like You* is Lauren's first novel. Find out more at LaurenStrasnick.com.